CEMETERY JONES AND THE DANCING GUNS

This time Sam—aptly known as "Cemetery"—Jones isn't the target. The bushwhacker who's taken a shot at Renee Hart, the woman bound to Sam, makes a run for the small but dangerous town dominated by one Cyrus Dunstan. That he'd harbor a killer who went after a woman is something for Sam to think hard about. But when Sam catches up with his quarry, he faces a whole army of folks for whom the death of Cemetery Jones means their ticket to glory.

Books by William R. Cox
in the Linford Western Library:

**THE GUNSHARP
CEMETERY JONES
CEMETERY JONES AND THE MAVERICK KID
CEMETERY JONES AND THE DANCING GUNS**

WILLIAM R. COX

CEMETERY JONES AND THE DANCING GUNS

Complete and Unabridged

LINFORD
Leicester

First published in the USA in 1987

First Linford Edition
published June 1990

British Library CIP Data

Cox, William. (William Robert), *1901*–
Cemetery Jones and the dancing guns.—
Large print ed.—
Linford western library
I. Title
813'.54[F]

ISBN 0-7089-6857-0

Published by
F. A. Thorpe (Publishing) Ltd.
Anstey, Leicestershire
Set by Rowland Phototypesetting Ltd.
Bury St. Edmunds, Suffolk
Printed and bound in Great Britain by
T. J. Press (Padstow) Ltd., Padstow, Cornwall

1

SAMUEL HORNBLOW JONES sat on the steps of the frame house he was allowing to be built for himself and pondered. How had he, the wanderer of the frontier, come to this?

The answer was inside the structure explaining to a dubious George Spade, undertaker and carpenter of the town of Sunrise, how plumbing could be built to carry water from the creek to the kitchen —and of all things, an indoor bathroom. She was a beautiful lady named Renee Hart. She subscribed to magazines from afar that had all kinds of newfangled fashions and designs.

Sam had acquired the property, acreage adjoining Sunrise, from Abe Solomon, the banker, as an investment. There was enough land to run a few cows, breed horses, even raise a crop. He had no interest in any of these projects. It was a pretty place, the creek running gay and cold from the hills, rolling gramma grass, clumps of pinon and rock oak and pine easy on the eye. The trouble was it would tie a man down to chores.

It was Renee who had prevailed upon him, asserting that hotel life was barren, that he needed room for his tack, which he had always stored at the livery stable, that he should have his own kitchen—where she could cook for him now and then. When he was with her this all seemed rational.

Her heels clicked as she came down the steps to sit beside him. She wore a man's shirt open at the throat, and pants made far from Sunrise that gave value to her long, slim legs. Her boots were high heeled. She wore her dark hair drawn back, caught by a barrette, and hanging to her waist. She was tall, broad shouldered with white, tapering hands. She played the piano in the class Sunrise saloon, El Sol. Where she came from no one knew or inquired. At the corners of her slanted onyx eyes were tiny, almost invisible lines divulging that she was not a girl—she was all woman.

She said, "George will come through." Her speech was eastern but softly natural. "He has the magazine plan."

"Can he read it?"

"Now, Sam. Your house will be a showplace."

"All I needed was a place for my stuff and sleepin' room. Adobe would've done it fine."

"Not good enough for a prominent citizen in a growing town. Even if he does spend half his time wandering around looking for trouble."

She had him there. His hated cognomen "Cemetery Jones" was truly earned. He had gained it in the course of the many adventures that he would far rather have avoided.

"Last thing I want is to be prominent," he muttered.

"You saved the bank—the town. You made your stake in the mine on those hills. You are part of Sunrise like it or not."

3

"Nothin' wrong with the town." He had been on the frontier all his life. He had gone up the trail—and learned to hate that work. He had been a gambler, a mine owner, and briefly a lawman. He was past thirty, which was elderly for a man whose gun had gained him the nickname "Cemetery", and he now wished to live quietly and enjoy Renee.

He was about to tell her this when the dog appeared.

Renee said, "Oh, the poor creature."

"Damn mutt's been in the crick." Sam had no great love for domestic animals. He did not even own a horse; he rented from livery stables.

Renee leaned forward as the creature approached at a tentative but determined pace. It was brindled dirty brown, of no pride in ancestry. Its ears hung listlessly almost to earth. Its hind legs seemed not coordinated with the front pair. Its huge brown eyes had accumulated sorrow. It paused, patently purposeful, conning them with surprising confidence.

The sun dipped toward the western

4

mountains, shadows lengthened. The dog spun and growled. Leaning to pet it, Renee lost her balance.

There was the sound of an angry bee, and the echo of a rifle shot rang out.

George Spade, coming from the house, stood still. Another bullet struck him in the shoulder. He said, "Geez, I'm hit."

Sam shoved at Renee, who rolled under the porch. Then he was running, Colt in hand, toward the pinon trees. Ahead of him the hound loped now swift and knowing as an arrow from a bow. The lush gramma grass deterred Sam but the hound never faltered on its appointed way.

Sam found it standing stiff-legged among fallen pinon nuts.

The sun did another fancy step and there was not enough light to read sign. The sound of hoofbeats going southward was far away. Sam's mind went around and around a frightening fact. The dog's head went down, its nose rooted, it looked up and whined.

Sam leaned down. There was a rifle

cartridge among the pinon nuts. He picked it up and said, "Dog, you're spooky, you know that?"

The dog wagged its tail. Sam went on, "It was like you knew that shot was comin'. Loco, dog, loco. It's like you know this shell could mean somethin'." He paused and lowered his voice as though someone might be eavesdropping. "Tell me this, do you know that shot wasn't meant for me? Hell, he coulda got me; I was a sittin' duck. He didn't fire until Renee got in his sights. Only for her goin' off balance there, he'd have got her, too."

He started back toward the house. The dog walked at his heels. He said, "You may be a haunt but I'll tell you what. You get washed up and then you get the best meal in town. And as many more as you can gobble."

Renee met them halfway. "Sam, you could have been shot. George is wounded in the shoulder."

"All I did was follow the dog. He knew the way."

6

"We have to get George to the doctor," she said.

Spade was white, gritting his teeth, holding his left arm with his right hand. "I can walk. Just come along with me, please."

They went slowly toward the main street of Sunrise. The dog stayed close to their heels. Sam never remembered the journey.

A look at the hole in the steps had told him that the bullet from the would-be assassin was definitely not meant for him.

Someone was gunning for Renee.

It had to be someone from her past, of which he knew nothing except that she had come from the East. She had arrived in town on the stage, unpacked her large, stylish wardrobe, and applied to Casey Robinson for a job playing in El Sol. She had settled in and converted the townsfolk to variations of the themes of the great composers, switching to lively popular tunes of the day at will. She was a fixture, beneficiary to local pride and admiration. Her affair with Sam went unnoted by the majority.

They had gravitated together on sight. Sam had been the owner of the Long John Mine, had sold it, and was thinking of moving along when he realized he was in love. The rest was history.

In the meantime there had been the troubles and then the growth of Sunrise, new houses, more businesses, a few kerosene street lights for the night-time. There was still raw scrambling taking place, of course. The rough element hung out in Rafferty's Saloon. Progress was not swift.

The bushwhacker who had shot at Renee had gone south, toward Dunstan, a smaller settlement thirty miles south of Sunrise. It was newer and rougher by far than Sunrise. Cyrus Dunstan, for whom it was named, was a tough former Texan, a grasping, egocentric man. He was banker, mayor, rancher, the whole shebang, Sam knew. That he would harbor a killer who would go after a woman was another matter. It was something to think hard about.

The trio reached Main Street and walked to Dr. Bader's office and hospital. At the same time Dr. Bader's self-designed vehicle rolled up. It was a miniature Conestoga wagon pulled by a gray cob. The driver's seat was made comfortable with padded leather, and there was room in the body for patients unable to walk. Dr. Bader peered at them, a stout man often the worse for liquor but apparently sober at this time.

"You have trouble?"

"George got shot out at my place," said Sam.

"So take him inside."

They did so. Sam said to George, "You'll be on payroll, you know. And send the doctor's bill to me."

"I'll do that," said Spade. "Hell, we'll never get your house built what with one thing and another."

"Don't fret," Sam told him.

Renee said, "Just so you get the arm back in use again."

9

She took Sam's elbow and they walked toward El Sol, where she had rooms above the saloon. She said calmly, "Someone tried to kill me."

He was not surprised that she knew. Most of the time she was far brighter than he. "Sure looks that way."

"He went south, didn't he?"

"Yep. I got a cartridge to look at. The dog pointed it."

The hound was still with them, had never left them for a moment. Renee leaned to pet him.

"We have to feed him. He's hungry."

"Looks like he's goin' to fall apart. He must've come a long way."

"With the shooter?"

"Could be. It was as if he knew the shot was coming."

Renee shivered. "It's a new experience for me."

They walked and the silence became uneasy. Finally Sam asked, "Who?"

"I haven't the faintest idea." She said it firmly and he knew she was telling the truth. He knew she had a past that included pain; the bond between them was so strong that they shared unspoken secrets, it seemed. There had been a man, or men; that was certain. He had no curiosity in that direction. The present had been enough for them—until now.

It was dark and Gimpy the lamplighter was doing his job. They came to El Sol and Sam said, "I'll be visitin' Dunstan."

"You will eat your supper," Renee said.

"Yeah, sure."

"And help me feed and care for the dog." She added, "We must give him a name."

"I'm no good at that. I got to get to Dunstan while the trail's still warm."

"I know you have to go." She was calm on the surface but there was turmoil in her, he knew.

"You're dead sure you haven't got a notion?" he asked.

"Sam, you know I'd tell you."

"I know."

"If I did, believe me . . . It's a scary matter, darling."

"More than that." They had come to Tolliver's Cafe. They went in and the dog followed them. Tolliver, a man of no nonsense, said, "Hey, I don't allow pets."

Sam said, "This is no pet. This is a hungry dog. What he needs is a bath and food. I'll just take him out back to your pump while you rustle up the grub."

"Now, Sam . . ." Tolliver scowled at the hound. It went to him and raised its muzzle and whimpered. He said, "Well . . . if it's your dog, Sam."

"He belongs to Miss Renee and me," Sam said. "Since he's the first I ever had I got to learn to take care of him."

Renee and Sam went out back and pumped water. The dog was not over-joyed but did not fight back. When the mud was washed from him he didn't look much better to Sam.

"He's ugly, you know that?"

The dog barked. Renee said, "Not ugly. Just . . . dog-like. A real dog."

"So maybe I wouldn't want a pretty dog," Sam said. "Where we goin' to keep him?"

"While you're away he'll stay with me. And very welcome he'll be," she said. "I'll need the company, Sam. I don't mind telling you I'm shaking, off and on. Mainly on."

"It'd be real strange if you were doing any different."

They sat at a table with the dog at their feet. Tolliver brought a platter of scraps and the hound sniffed it, then nosed it with surprising delicacy.

Tolliver took their order of the regular dinner, roast beef, mashed potatoes and gravy, coffee and apple pie with home-made ice cream. Sam ate heartily, but Renee picked at the food and was silent. When they had finished Sam paid the bill, and they walked across to El Sol, the dog at their heels. Casey Robinson, who owned both the saloon and the hotel, met them, cocking an eye.

"Where'd that come from?"

"That is a dog named . . . well, plain Dog," Sam said. "For now he belongs to Renee. You got any arguments?"

"Hell, no," said Robinson. "I like

dogs. He is a real dog, ain't he?" The dog growled and took a step toward him. "Hey, I'm only kiddin'. Gosh, you'd think he understood me."

"Don't bet against it," Sam told him. Upstairs, the dog looked around Renee's room and settled down, head on paws. It was a room she had furnished for herself. The bed was large and soft. There were two deep, comfortable chairs, and Navajo rugs adorned the floor. A pair of windows looked out on the street. Paintings unfamiliar to western eyes hung on the walls. A wardrobe had been built along one side of the room. It was filled with garments not purchased in Sunrise.

Renee sank into one of the chairs. "Sam?"

"Yeah?"

"Sam, I don't want you to ride down to Dunstan tonight."

"I got to get goin'."

"Not tonight, Sam, please."

"The trail's getting cold." He thought of the cartridge shell that the dog had turned up. He took it from his pocket and examined it under the light of Renee's bright oil lamp. It was a .44, and on the perimeter of brass there was a noticeable nick. The hammer of the rifle that had fired the shot was slightly damaged. Therefore it could be identified.

The problem was to find that particular rifle in a country where every man owned one.

She said, "I don't want to be alone."

"You got the dog."

It was lying with its head on its paws, ears trailing, eyes wide and fastened on Renee. As Sam spoke, its tail wagged, thumping the floor.

She said, "That may not be a joke. He's a special dog."

"Dunstan," said Sam. "There's somethin' about that town. Like an apple rotten at the core."

"I've never been there."

"Passin' through, it stinks around the edges. It's a good bet the shooter either comes from there—or stopped there on his way."

"I know you're going there. I don't see

how you can learn anything in a place like that."

"Can't learn anything stayin' here." He understood her objections. She was carefully hiding shock and fear. "I'll have people lookin' after you."

"No," she said. "I don't want to be a burden. People could be killed looking after me. I won't have it."

He said, "Renee. Sweetheart, this is your town. You're part and parcel of Sunrise. This is the West, not one of your eastern cities. Your friends will want to watch out for you."

"Please don't bring them into it," she begged.

"I ain't about to make an announcement. But George is wounded. I can't shut him up. It'll get out one way or another. George is no fool. He saw the bullet hole. He knows the shots weren't for me."

She shook her head. He put his arms around her and went on, "All right. I'll stay tonight. Let's go downstairs and make believe and see what happens."

"It's hard to make believe right now." But she composed herself and applied rice powder and a touch of pink to her face. The dog watched her as though perplexed at such unnecessary adornment.

Sam went to a closet where he had stored an arm holster that he had seldom used. He removed his gun belt and thrust his revolver into the holster, concealing it beneath a lightweight jacket. It was against the rules of El Sol to wear a gun within the premises, but he felt the occasion warranted it. If nothing happened no one would be the wiser.

Renee said, "I'm making believe," and they went down the stairs and into the busy saloon. The dog never left their heels.

It was the night for the weekly poker game among the town fathers, Mayor Wagner, Ted Tillus, Morgan Keene, and Casey Robinson. Sam said his hellos and Shaky the bartender brought a whiskey glass for him as he joined the action. It was a modest game played for fun rather than profit, dollar limit, straight poker, nothing wild, stud or draw.

Renee sat at the piano and played her swinging variations of classical themes. Sam, through her instruction, had learned to detect the origin of the tunes. She was playing Bach, which was her sad music.

Mayor Wagner asked, "What in hell is that?" pointing to the hound at Sam's feet.

"A dog," Sam said.

"What you doin' with such a dilapidated critter?"

"He likes me," Sam said.

"Where did you get it?"

"Out of nowhere into the here," quoted Sam from a half-remembered lullaby.

He looked at his hand. He had a four flush in spades. He raised before the draw, drew the black queen, and won the pot. He said, "Dog brings me luck, y'see?"

"You always have the luck," Tillus said.

Sam had learned gambling from Luke Short, a friend from the Dodge City days now residing in Fort Worth. That was all anyone needed to know, since Short was the premier card man of his time. Sam could hold his own from table stakes to penny ante.

Casey Robinson, who had held a high straight against Sam's flush, said, "You ain't aimin' to keep him in the hotel, are you?"

The dog got to its feet. It stared at Robinson, then waddled over to the piano and flopped down near Renee.

Sam said, "Best be careful what you say around him."

"Humph, you wouldn't be complainin' if Sam wasn't movin' out of your hotel," said Mayor Wagner.

"Yeah," Tillus said. "It's a real ugly mutt, but a man's dog is a man's dog."

Morgan Keene said, "Since we're the city council you're outvoted, Casey. Though I do hope it's house broke."

"It's damn near human," Sam told him.

Robinson stared at the hound and the hound stared back. "I dunno. We got rules." He got up from the table and walked to the piano. The hound bared its teeth briefly. Casey said, "Hell, don't stay mad at me."

The dog slowly rose. It took two wobbly steps and rubbed against Robinson's leg, then returned to its place at Renee's feet. Robinson scratched his head.

"Hell—'scuse me, Miss Renee—can he talk, too?"

"Not yet," Sam told him. "We're workin' on that."

Now everyone was laughing and making conversation about Sam's peculiar dog. Renee broke into "Camptown Races" and the girls—there were two, Betsy and Rita, who did not go upstairs but might be persuaded to go elsewhere with a good customer—were soon whirling around as the poker game continued. Music hath charms, and all, thought Sam. He had a bit of music within him, he had found, without the ability to give it voice. It was nice, having music. The dog's tail beat the barroom floor, keeping perfect time.

Adam Burr, the Jerseyite turned western bank officer, and his wife, Peggy, entered and joined the throng circling the floor. It was, after all, Saturday night, Sam remembered. He watched the young couple fondly; they were as close to family as he owned. The hand was stud poker, and he idly threw in a call against Casy Robinson's pair of queens showing and got a quick raise. He met the raise, drew an ace to match one in the hole, and again the hotel owner bit the dust.

Robinson did not holler. He leaned over and stared into the eyes of the hound and said, "Hey, now, no hard feelin's, huh?"

The dog stuck out its long tongue and seemed to actually grin. Robinson sighed. "Guess it'll take time."

Sam said to the dog, "He owns the joint. Be nice to the man."

Robinson won the next two hands. Now everyone wanted to pet the hound, who retreated beneath Sam's chair and snapped at all advancers until they good-naturedly ceased.

The music stopped. Peggy Burr went to Renee, and Adam came to pat Sam's shoulder and be introduced to the hound.

"Ha'nted, it is," said Robinson. "You should name it Ha'nt."

"No way," said Sam. "Name of Dog, just plain Dog. Answers to that, seems to like it."

Adam Burr, once of Princeton University in New Jersey, said, "It is certainly Sam's dog and his prerogative to name it."

So that was decided. The dance ended, the customers returned to the bar or to tables, at one of which Renee and the Burrs seated themselves with libations.

Into this peaceful scene burst three young men, swaggering to the bar. That they were strangers, that Marshal Donovan had not encountered them on his rounds was proven by the fact that they wore guns at their belts. They also wore long stemmed spurs that jingle-jangle-jingled and fancy shirts and very tight Levis and two-toned boots not fit to ride a range. They shoved their way to the bar and one immediately recognized as the leader, a husky blond youth, demanded loudly, "Hey, where's the music and the gals?" as he threw a gold piece on the mahogany.

The hound came awake and was on its feet, pointing. Sam said, "Down, Dog. This ain't your play."

The dog remained stiff and ready. There was a shocked silence in the saloon.

Shaky steadied his palsied hands on the bar and said, "You check your guns in this here town, pilgrim."

"You mean we got the only guns in the joint? Hiyu!" The blond youth yanked out a long barreled, pearl handled Colt .45 and fired a shot into the ceiling, bawling, "Now let's get this party started, people!"

Sam turned in his chair. No one actually saw him draw. The fancy revolver flew out of the stranger's hand. He spun around, howling in pain. Sam fired a second shot. It took off one of the fancy spurs. The stranger staggered, and by that time Adam Burr had crossed the room. When the offender came around, Adam hit him with a perfect right cross to the jaw, knocking him sliding to the floor.

The remaining two, who upon closer examination turned out to be identical twins, cried in unison, "Not us! We told the Kid not to start somethin'."

Marshal Donkey Donovan came through the door. "What in tarnation's goin' on here? Can't I turn my back without some clown actin' up?"

Mayor Wagner said, "No problem, Marshal. Jail's empty so far as I know."

The twins howled, "Not us. Please, we don't mean no harm."

Donovan snarled, "What's your name?"

"Olsen," they chorused. "Oley and Sven. Olsen. We're from Dunstan."

"That figures," the marshal said. "And who's he?"

"Kid Dunstan. The mayor's son. He had too much booze. We told him."

Their voices blended. They held their hands shoulder high, blinking.

Sam was reloading his gun. "Dunstan, huh? Maybe it's best I took him home tomorrow, since I'm goin' that way."

"Better you than me," said the mayor. "Why do you want to visit that hell hole?"

Sam dissembled. "Just a notion. Wake him up. Put him away. Fine him and I'll take him over."

"Best way," agreed Wagner. "Fifty dollars and damages."

The big blond kid was sitting up, rubbing his jaw, staring wildly around. Donovan dragged him to his feet. He mumbled, "My old man'll getcha for this. I was only funnin'. He'll getcha, wait and see."

The marshal shook him and said, "Yeah. You tell your old man Cemetery Jones only shot away your gun and your spur and he'll send thanks to heaven."

"I don't care who . . ." He stopped and gulped, staring at Sam. "Uh— Cemetery Jones?"

"Now he can brag all over his dirty little town about how he faced Sam. Shoulda shot his butt off," Wagner said.

The twins now pleaded, "Can we go to jail with him? His paw'll kill us if we come home without him."

"If you can pay for your night's lodgin'," Donovan said. "No free beds for the likes of you."

"We'll pay. We'll be right glad to pay," they chorused.

"That's a vaudeville act," Renee said. "They should go on the stage."

"It's a rare phenomenon," Adam Burr said. "Twins who think in tandem. But it's a matter of record that they exist."

"Yeah. There they are," said Mayor Wagner. "And there they go like little lambs."

As Donovan prodded the trio out of El Sol, Renee returned to the piano. The evening wore on almost as though nothing had happened. Not too long ago it would have meant even less to the citizens of Sunrise, Sam though. Times were changing.

As the customers were dancing there was the horn and the rattle of the evening stage arriving. Several citizens left to meet it. Renee took another break. The poker game broke up as Tillus and Morgan quit. Sam joined the Burrs at their table, along with Renee.

In through the doors came a tall, thin young man. He wore funeral black. His collar, soiled from traveling, was turned backwards. He had a shock of red hair and was quite handsome. He spoke in a clear, resonant voice.

"I was told I could find Adam Burr in here."

Adam rose and stared. "Clayton Lomax? Is it really you?"

"None other." The newcomer strode, bright-eyed, beaming, hands outstretched. "I thought I'd never get here."

"Wha-what are you doing here?" Adam took the hands, wrung them, turned to face the suddenly silent crowd. "This is a classmate of mine from school. He was Princeton Divinity."

"A priest and he's a friend of yours?" Mayor Wagner chuckled.

"Presbyterian," said Adam. "He'll have a cold beer, Shaky."

The newcomer was introduced all around. He sat down at the table and said, "I expect to be viewed with suspicion. I understand you have no church in Sunrise."

Adam said, "You know because I wrote to you."

Clayton Lomax rubbed his thatch of flaming hair. He said, reproachfully, "You didn't tell me how rough it is in the West, you know. I lost my hat on the last stop. Town of Dunstan. Fellow shot it off. Didn't like preachers."

"You let him get away with that?" demanded Adam.

"Oh, no. I chastised him." Lomax showed a swollen left hand.

Adam explained, "Clay and I boxed some in school."

"And I'm not exactly Presbyterian," the newcomer said. "I'm more—uh— nondenominational. Got the idea the Lord loves us all. If you know what I mean. So it seemed best I find a new territory."

Mayor Wagner moved from his table. "Could you teach school, Lomax? Kids, like?"

Adam coughed. "Well, you see—uh—we thought, Peggy and I—if we had a child, there's no real school here. So I wrote to Clay."

Peggy said, "Well, it's true. And a church—it would be better than the Ladies Sewing Circle and all."

Mayor Wagner said, "You're hired, stranger. A school and a church, this town can build 'em. Sunrise is gettin' plumb civilized. Ain't a soul in town this side of Rafferty's Saloon won't welcome you."

Clayton Lomax grinned, showing even white teeth. "Just like that?"

"You're in the West, man," Adam said, delighted. He pulled out a fat wallet. "I've been saving a thousand dollars to start the church and school. And I'm donating the land for it."

The mayor said, "I'll put up another thousand. And you'll board with me."

Lomax said, "Whew," and drank his beer in one gulp. "Adam, you were right. It's a sudden country."

Shaky brought another beer. The time passed as people came to greet the newest addition to the town. Somehow Sam Jones felt lost. Church and school were not in his immediate ken. He accepted them as valuable but he was a stranger to institutions. The country was changing before his eyes in many ways. And someone was out to kill Renee Hart.

She played for the preacher and he got up and sang "Nearer My God To Thee" and some joined in the chorus, but Sam did not know the words. The hound slept through it all.

When it was over and everyone departed and Shaky was cleaning up, Renee and Sam went upstairs to her apartment. The hound followed, sniffed around the hallway, looked hard at them, then settled down, head on ungainly paws.

Sam said, "You and me, Dog. Reckon we're dyin' out, all these newfangled things happening."

"A preacher who drinks beer and knocks gunmen about is a novelty but not liable to make you feel outdated. And we do need a school," Renee said.

"Certain." Sam nodded. He closed the door and she came into his arms and she was shaking a bit. He said, "Now take it easy. There's nobody goin' to harm you whilst I'm alive."

"Oh, Sam, you know the next shot would have been for you. I just can't understand why he didn't get you first."

"He wanted to bag us both. The hound must've confused him some."

"He wasn't bright. That doesn't make him less dangerous. If he came from Dunstan there must be someone or something behind him."

"That's why I'm goin' down there tomorrow," Sam said.

"With those brats. I'm sure they couldn't have anything to do with it. They're too young and callow."

31

"Dunstan's spoiled kid and the tandem brothers? No, they couldn't be trusted to do the job."

She said, "I'm not afraid to die, Sam. That doesn't mean I'm ready. And I can't bear the idea of taking you down with me."

"Who me? Are you funnin' me? Nobody takes me down."

"Famous last words." But she relaxed and went to the table and poured two tiny vials of the brandy she often received from the East. It was very aromatic, and he had learned to sip it with full appreciation.

He said, "That dog, now. That was plumb strange."

"He's one of us."

Sam had never thought of himself as peculiar. True, he had been through more escapades than was normal, but he had always accepted life as it came, asking no odds, giving none. It was all part of living on the frontier, he reckoned.

He said only, "Maybe you're right. It'll work out. Things always do."

"In the end. There has to be an end. Very few people get out of this world alive."

"Nor takes anything with 'em." He laughed and she joined him and he kissed her. When they were alone together it was always like this.

2

SAM was awake at dawn, slipping out of El Sol by the rear door while Renee slept, obeying the customs of the time. He went to his room at the hotel and changed clothing, cleaned his gun and strapped it low on his thigh and tied it down. He walked to the livery stable and saddled a black horse called Midnight, a rangy, swift steed he had hired before. He had breakfast at Tolliver's and bought cold food for the trip to Dunstan.

Donkey Donovan was ready with the prisoners, who were subdued, acquiescent to every demand. The protuberant blue eyes of young Dunstan stayed upon Sam, watching his every move. The boys wore their guns and belts, empty of ammunition. The pearl-handled revolver was battered and did not quite fit the holster.

The marshal said, "I should be doin' this job my own self."

"They're goin' my way." Sam shrugged. "No trouble."

Donovan winked at him. "Sure. Only they might get smart on you and get themselves killed, the way you are."

"Could be." Sam returned the wink and marched the prisoners to the livery stable where they were forced to pay for the night's lodging of their horses. Young Dunstan opened his mouth to protest, then closed it as his gaze fell upon Sam's tied-down sidearm.

They began the journey. As they passed El Sol the hound came loping and fell into their wake. Sam reined in. He leaned down and said slowly and distinctly, "Dog, you stay. You take care of Renee, savvy?"

There was a long moment, a clash of wills. Then the dog lowered its head, turned, and went back to the saloon. Its tail however, did not drag, and it did not look back at Sam, behavior quite unlike that of a hound who has been reproved.

Sam caught up with the prisoners who rode mustangs, he noted, ordinary cattle horses. He rode far enough behind to evade the cloud of dust from the trio, leaving them to their own devices, having no desire to speak with them. He and young Dunstan were eons apart, not only in age but in fundamentals, he knew. The kid was the descendant of a dying breed. If another killer didn't get them they might survive; most of their kind had not in the hard days after the War. Law and order had to come, but sometimes it seemed to interfere with what a man had been taught to believe.

For instance a small hurrah such as had been started last night by the Dunstan boy might have gone down with a laugh and a round of drinks in another time and place. Maybe even in El Sol a couple of years ago. Maybe he had been too quick to act—he often pondered his sudden moves, made without conscious thought.

Now it was something people expected of him, he supposed. "Cemetery Jones" —he hated the nickname. He had acquired it in those other days and had faced men who challenged it—not him but the inference of the label "Cemetery". He had killed defending himself. He had never been sought by the law. Yet he nurtured doubts, often, about the killing.

The sun rose hot and bright, and it became noon, and he called to the youths ahead to stop by a convenient small stream trickling down from the hills that bordered the road. He passed out food, and the twins in their odd chorus thanked him, and Kid Dunstan grunted but ate like the others. Of conversation there was none.

Sam studied the trio, sitting apart. They handled their horses well, unbridling, allowing them to drink and to nibble, but they lacked the facility of working stiffs. He tried to differentiate between the Olsen twins, thought he detected that one's head was a slightly different shape and that they were not identical in size and weight by a fraction. He could not, however, tell which was which by name, since they did not call each other by name, nor in any other way. They communicated without words. Young Dunstan seemed not in the mood to speak with anyone, and Sam decided that might be all for the best.

Soon they were on the road again. There was now a bit of traffic on the way, wagons bearing supplies, farmers riding hayloads, horsemen bent on various errands. Some were known to Sam, some to the boys. No one seemed curious. It became late afternoon, hot but with a breeze blowing. It seemed to Sam that the young men were tiring. They lacked the muscles gained by hard labor, he suspected.

There was a curve to the road and the breeze blew up a dust cloud. Sam lost sight of his charges as he wiped his eyes with his rebosa. When he could see again there was a group of riders, four men surrounding the kids, the Dunstan boy's arm waving.

The quartet all wore navy blue shirts and flat black hats. There was an obvious leader, a straight-backed, tall fellow with a hard, square jaw and piercing dark eyes, all of which Sam took in with instinctive thoroughness. He walked the horse toward them, loosening his rifle in its scabbard.

The blue-shirted leader swung around and faced him, scowling, "You, there. Stop and talk."

Sam said, "Talk about what?"

"What is your standing? Are you a lawman?"

"Not exactly. Kinda fillin' in for the marshal of Sunrise," Sam said easily. "And you?"

"Captain Steve Fisher."

"You wearin' a star?"

"I'm acting in the interest of Mayor Dunstan."

"Lookin' for the wanderin' boy? He got himself in a bit of trouble last night."

"You fired upon him."

"Nope."

"He says you did."

"Captain," Sam said, "if I truly fired at him he wouldn't be here now, would he?"

"That's neither here nor there . . ."

Sam interrupted, "Take my word for it."

The twins exploded, "That's Cemetery Jones."

"Never heard the name," Captain Fisher said. "Mayor Dunstan will want to see you, sir."

"Well, it so happens I aim to see Mayor Dunstan. Should we get along with it?"

The other three men from Dunstan had their hands on their guns. They seemed ordinary riders, very much of the same ilk, neither ugly nor fair. They did not seem aggressive. Evidently they had heard of Cemetery Jones.

Captain Fisher said, "These young men are now in my care. You can do what you like."

"They might be in your care, but they go before the mayor when we get in town," Sam told him. "You just mosey along. I'll be right with you."

The Dunstan boy yelped, "You see? You see how he is? He's got no right."

"Comes a time when might makes

right," Sam said. "You got the numbers there. Anybody want to start a ruckus? It ain't necessary. Dyin' on a nice day like this is a sad proposition."

He spoke with a smile but there was in his voice a warning. It got home to the three men in blue who followed Captain Fisher. He recognized it at once, saw the Captain hesitate, saw that the man was not afraid, that he had the instinct and the brains to accept a standoff.

"No need to talk of dying," Fisher said stiffly. "I was asked to look for the boys. Shall we now proceed to town?"

"Like you say." A military man, no question of it, Sam thought. The uniforms of the followers were thus explained. Something new in Dunstan, something to ponder.

For the remainder of the way young Dunstan rode with Captain Fisher and talked, receiving little response. The twins remained silent, as did the three blue clad riders. Sam followed, alert but silent.

Dunstan had added a new small hotel,

he found, but was still a one-street town, adobe shacks huddled together around two saloons, a general store, a hay and feed shop next to a barber's emporium. The Dunstan house at the far end of the avenue was of wood and plaster, sticking out like a sore thumb. City Hall was a large, rambling building which acommodated a jail in the rear and a large empty room that would be used for meetings. Dunstan was raw and it could be a dangerous place for a stranger, especially one with the message that Sam had to carry.

Cyrus Dunstan, it turned out, was at home. Night was falling when they arrived at the door. A large dusky woman answered the door.

Captain Fisher said, "Itha. Permission to speak to the mayor."

"Lawsy, is that you, Danny Dunstan?" She peered at the assorted crew and stepped inside. "Your pa is gonna give you fits, stayin' out all night without givin' notice. You Olsen boys, it's a good thing your folks is away. I swan, I dunno what young uns is comin' to these days."

They entered through a small hall and turned into a huge room filled with the most garish mail order furniture Sam had ever seen. Once indoors young Dunstan seemed to grow a foot. He commanded, "Mind your own business, Itha, and call my mom."

At the far end of the room a tiny woman stood, stared, then came forward calling, "Cy! There's folks here to see you."

"They put me in jail, Mom," her son wailed. "This here fella shot my new gun all to pieces and ruined my spurs. I was jus' funnin' and they jumped me and hit me."

A roar came from another room, "What's this? What the hell is goin' on? You there Cap?"

Fisher responded, "Yes, sir. There's a man from Sunrise has another tale to tell, I fear."

The man who came into the room was big. He was tall and wide and thick through the middle. His face was craggy, his mouth wide beneath a bushy mustache. He was dressed in ill-fitting city garments but wore broken-in cowboy boots. He rumbled, "I betcha there's another story to tell."

"Now, Cy," said his wife. "Don't you be listenin' to slander on your own son."

"My son." The big man's head wagged. He spotted Sam. He said, "Ho, there. You in on this?"

"I brought 'em back here."

"Cemetery Jones. You do the shootin' he's yammerin' about?"

"Yep."

Cy Dunstan eyed his son. "You sorry pup, you're lucky to be alive and standing there. I seen this man work in Dodge City when you were a squallin' brat. I seen Masterson and I seen Earp and they can't hold a candle to him. You . . ."

Mrs. Dunstan threw her arms around the boy and cried, "No! It couldn't happen to my darlin'. Don't you talk like that."

Sam was watching Captain Fisher out

of the corner of his eye. He saw the prominent jaw muscle bulge, he saw his hand dart to the butt of his gun. He knew the symptoms, they were all certain they were the fastest.

Dunstan said without raising his already loud voice, "Never mind that now, woman. You twins, you go home and don't you leave the house 'til I say so." He waited until the boys had hastily departed. "They tag along. Any trouble, I know who caused it. Cap, what you got to say?"

Stiffly, Fisher said, "It is a matter of who to believe."

Now Dunstan grinned, showing strong, yellow teeth, "Jones, you got to 'scuse the captain. He's kinda new. Keeps order, teaches the young uns somewhat. We're gonna make this town bigger and better'n Sunrise. I'm promisin' you."

"Sounds good." The man loved to hear himself talk, Sam thought.

Dunstan turned to Fisher. "As for you, when it comes to military doin's and so forth I don't augur. But when it comes down to that boy against Cemetery Jones —I know 'em both. Leastways I know about Jones from hearsay. He don't lie."

His wife shrilled, "Cy, don't you make my darlin' a fibber."

"The good Lord done that." Still he did not speak unkindly. He was merely stating the truth as he saw it, Sam recognized. He now asked, "What's the damages?"

"All paid."

Dunstan shook his massive head. "Givin' him cash to carry again. I told you and told you."

Mrs. Dunstan said, "We've got the money. Why shouldn't my boy have fun?"

"Shootin' off his mouth when he's totin' iron is mighty dangerous fun," Dunstan said, as if explaining to a child. "Here I am tryin' to make this town a decent place and he goes to Sunrise and causes us to look like trash. Fisher, you do somethin' about this, you hear? I want his ass worked. I want him to learn how to act in decent comp'ny."

"Yes, sir." The tone was colorless. The man felt he was losing face, Sam knew. He could be a very dangerous man indeed, working with the youths of Dunstan. It was plain that he was not entirely in agreement with Dunstan, probably held him in contempt.

"We're goin' to do things, I tell you," Dunstan insisted. "We got plans."

As if on cue, a female figure appeared at the head of the stairway to the second story of the big house. She was diminutive, blonde, clad in a long gown that had never been purchased in Dunstan—nor in Sunrise. Sam recognized it as the sort that Renee wore, except that this one was low cut to reveal the contours of breasts larger than seemed proper on such a small woman. When she slowly descended the stairs she seemed to float, her fingertips scarcely touching the banister. She came across the floor as if on wheels, smiling, head cocked to one side. She had a small nose and a rather large but shapely mouth and pearly teeth. She was the epitome of grace and extreme style.

Sam could feel the temperature of the room rise. The brat Kid was beaming. Captain Fisher stood more erect than before, if that were possible. Mrs. Dunstan uttered a little squeal of pleasure. Only Cy Dunstan seemed un-affected except in his delivery, a small roar.

"Just what I was talkin' on. Miss Vera Brazile, meet Cem . . ."

Sam, fed up, interrupted, "If you don't mind, Mayor, my name is Sam Jones."

For a moment it seemed that Dunstan would be annoyed. Then he beamed and said, "Sartain, sartain, Mr. Sam Jones from Sunrise. A neighbor you might say. He's invited to the swaree, whenever it comes off."

The woman did her glide over to offer Sam a limp hand. He imagined she thought he would kiss it. She had that effect. He touched it and said, "Pleased, I'm sure."

"Cotillion," she said. Her voice was melodious. "With the help of the mayor and his gracious lady I have brought the

48

new dances—and new music—to this great western country, I do hope and pray."

"From New y'Orleans," Dunstan said triumphantly. "None of your knee high stompin' and swingin' around. Real class dancin'. The waltz. You ever seen a waltz, Jones?"

"I've had the pleasure." He was being too damned polite, he thought, especially since he was not being sincere. He was looking for an assassin, not social pleasantries.

"I find western people naturally graceful," said Vera Brazile. "In no time at all they catch onto the rhythm."

"Yes, ma'am." Sam had seen a heap of dancing from Indian tribal to the hug-em-up of bordellos. To imagine a cotillion in Dunstan taxed his belief.

"Perhaps you would attend the class tonight, Mr. Jones?"

Dunstan bellowed, "Right! Give you chance to see what's what in this here burg. Just about suppertime. Set with us?"

Sam said, "I'm sorry, but I've got a couple errands."

"Later, then. You can't go home tonight. It's at the City Hall, you know, the big room."

"Maybe," Sam said. He bowed to the ladies. "I'll be on my way now."

Dunstan followed him to where his horse stood at the hitching rail. He said, "I'm tellin' you true, Sam Jones, we're gonna catch up with Sunrise and beat it."

"Might be." Sam paused. "Wanted to tell you, though. A bushwhacker took a shot at me yesterday. Headed this way. Maybe you got some notions?"

"Bushwhacked you? Hell no. I'm tryin' to keep the peace. Got enough trouble with that brat of mine."

"If you hear anything I'd appreciate it," Sam said.

"If I hear anything I'll have Fisher take care of him," promised Dunstan. "Damn any bushwhacker ever lived."

"Thanks. Later, maybe." Sam mounted and rode into the early night.

At the hotel, which was clean, if primitive, he asked the owner, "You know where the Olsens live?"

"Right around the corner. Olsen's the butcher. Outa town buyin' beef right now. Him and his missus."

"Thanks. Can I get a meal here?"

"Well . . . my wife could run up something." He was a clean-shaven man named Dixon. "Put your horse in the stable? I got no help, have to do it all yourself."

"Thanks, I'll take the vittles and fodder for the horse." He went out to the street. People were moving about; there was a lot of noise from the saloons. A woman lurched into him and said in a whiskey voice, "Buy me a drink, stranger? I'll show you a good time."

He said, "No, thanks," and reached for the bridle of the black horse.

A man growled, "Insultin' a lady, you bastid?" and came at him with a short, heavy club. Always chary of hurting his gun hand, Sam hooked with his left elbow and nailed the attacker on the chin. As the man went down he kicked him in the crotch.

The woman clawed, screeching. He slapped her across the back of her neck and knocked her onto the prone pimp.

He said, "Now don't you two try to get up for ten minutes. And don't see me later."

He led the horse to the barn behind the hotel and cared for him. The barn was clean and neat by lantern light. It was a town of contrasts, he thought, like every other frontier burg he had known over the years.

He ate a quick, good meal and paid for it, adding his compliments. He walked around the corner as he'd been directed and found an adobe house of ample dimensions. There was a light in the kitchen, and he tapped on the window. The Olsen twins appeared as if on strings and stared at him. After a moment they beckoned him to the rear door. The were owl-eyed but not frightened when he entered.

He said, "Wanted to palaver some."

"Okay, Mr. Jones." Now they were a bit off key, as though speaking to a person in their own home made a difference.

He asked, "Now which of you is which? By name, that is."

They exchanged quick glances. Then the one with the narrower head said, "Nobody ever asks that. I'm Sven. He's Oley."

It was a huge kitchen, immaculate. Sam helped himself to a chair and asked, "You boys dress alike to fool people?"

Sven said, "It's our ma."

Oley said, "She always did it to us." Now it could be heard that his voice was in a slightly different key than that of Sven.

Sven said, "We just always have."

"You ride with young Dunstan a lot?"

"No," they chorused. "Mainly when Cap Fisher drills us."

"I see." He had thought they were not of the same stamp as the braggart Kid. "You like this Fisher's outfit?"

53

Sven hesitated and then said, "Everybody's in it. Like military."

"A young army."

"Uh—some of the older fellas are gettin' into it, too, when they have time."

"Anybody from out of town?"

Sven said, "A couple. Kinda rough. Like army fellas."

"Who you goin' to fight?"

"Oh, Injuns. Robbers. Like that. Be prepared, Cap always says."

"Real good. If there were any Indians on the warpath or any robber gangs around. Your pa lets you off from work to train thisaway?"

"That's right. We work in the shop. It's the only one in town."

Sam asked, "These new fellas, where do they work?"

"Oh, Mr. Dunstan gave them jobs on the ranch when Cap asked him to."

"Cap Fisher—he's the town marshal?"

"We ain't got one. Mayor Dunstan said we don't need one since we're all sorta watchin' over things." Sven seemed a bit

54

uncertain. "All this dancin' and stuff, the town's changin'."

"You don't cotton to the dancin'?"

"We like it. Papa does. He's Swedish. Ma, she's Scottish. She wishes for a church."

Sam said, "Tell your ma we're gettin' a church in Sunrise. We got dancin', too, in El Sol."

They were puzzled. "Pa's got good business here."

"Him and Mr. Dunstan are good friends," Sven said.

"I see. You boys satisfied the way you were treated in Sunrise?"

They chorused again, "It was fair. Kid, he caused it all. We got treated okay."

"Thanks, boys." Sam got up to leave. At the door he paused and asked, "You seen anything of a clumsy old hound dog around these parts?"

The giggled. Sven said, "Sure did. Few days ago he bit Kid Dunstan. Kid fired at him and missed. Kid, he ain't much of a shot, truly."

"Glad I asked."

Sven said soberly, "Mr. Jones."

"Yeah?"

"Cap Fisher, they say he's the fastest gun in the West. We seen him draw. He's tremendous good."

"Why are you tellin' me?"

"Uh—you were mighty quick last night. And you treated us fair and square."

"Reckon you're warnin' me."

They hesitated, then said together, "We don't like Cap Fisher much."

"You know, I agree," said Sam. "Okay, is there a way around the back, past the hotel, then to the street?"

"We'll show you."

"No. Just tell me."

They went to the back with him and pointed the way, which was dark and deserted. He said, "See you at the dance," and moved quietly and cautiously. He found the alley they had indicated and prowled to the main street.

As he had expected, they were waiting. They were covering the hotel entrance, the pimp, crouched and still in pain, and several others, lurking in doorways and the mouth of the alley next to the street where the Olsens dwelt. He pondered a moment.

He should not kill anyone in Dunstan. Fisher would be on him in a moment. On the other hand this crew would bludgeon him to death and vanish into the woodwork, and there would be little time spent looking for them. He could run for it and risk a gauntlet, but that was not his style. He drew a deep breath and walked out onto the street, lit only by lights from the buildings and the hotel. He stayed close to the buildings.

They came like a pack of rats, swinging clubs. He saw the glint of a blade. He waited, singled out the knife man. He fired low. The man screamed and went down. They made the error of coming abreast. He fanned the Colt, a procedure which did not allow for aim. He shot at their legs, moving as he fired. Sidling, he emptied the gun and, from long practice, reloaded. One came close; he kicked out. Then, suddenly, those who were not howling in pain were gone, like rats to their holes.

And there was Captain Fisher and several men. They were not wearing their uniform blue; they were dressed for the dance at City Hall. He waited at the entrance to the hotel.

Fisher said, "What is this, sir?"

"You tell me," Sam said, holstering his gun.

"Why did you shoot these men?"

"To keep them from killin' me," Sam said. "You got a real bad bunch around here, Captain. Whores, pimps, a sorry lot."

"No reason to shoot them down like dogs."

"Dogs? Way I see it, dogs are more decent."

"I'll have to put you under arrest, Jones."

Sam moved one step, facing Fisher. "I don't reckon so."

"You defy the law?"

"I claim self defense. Also I wonder

where you were when all this was goin' on? This gatherin' of trash."

Now from the side street came the Olsen twins. They said in their duet style, "We seen it all, Cap. They come at him with clubs and knives. He coulda killed 'em. He shot low. We seen him."

One of the Fisher's followers had been examining the victims. He called, "That's right, Cap. Every damn one is shot below the middle."

Sam said, "Be best to call the doctor and then sashay on down to the dance, wouldn't it, Captain Fisher?"

There was one second when he thought the man would test him with his fast draw. Then it was gone, postponed, he thought, to a future date.

Fisher ordered two of his crew, "Go for the doctor. Hold these people for questioning. I'll talk to you later, Jones," he added.

"Talk to me right now. I see the emporium across the street is lighted. I'll bet you could get it opened for me. Have to buy a fresh shirt for the dance, y'see."

Fisher hesitated—and was lost. Those behind him were intent, listening. He waved to them. "Go along. Help clean up this mess and then go to the dance."

Sam walked across the street with him, and Fisher rapped on the door locked against violence. A man peered out, then admitted them.

Sam said, "I'll need a shirt and some underwear." He turned to Fisher. "Maybe you can help. Some joker tried to ambush me in Sunrise yesterday. You got anybody like that around?"

"What do you mean, sir?" Fisher scowled.

"Anybody you could suspect? Might have rode out day before yesterday, returned today?"

"I can't keep watch on everyone in town. Consider what just happened. It will take time to clear out the rats."

"And you're new here."

"Comparatively." The captain talked in a clipped accent, not southern, not true Yankee.

"Just thought I'd ask." Sam selected a

dark red flannel shirt and light underwear. "I'll be gone early tomorrow, so if you got anything to say, go to it."

Fisher cleared his throat. "In view of the statements of the Olsen boys there will be no charges. Have you information as to who began the attack?"

"A pimp. The big bastid who got one in the knee. He didn't give me his name when he and his whore came at me earlier. Just gathered some pardners and waited for me."

"I think I know who you mean," Fisher said. "I will take steps."

"You do that. Don't let me keep you from the party," Sam said. "You all prettied up and everything."

Fisher was attired in a gray serge suit with highly polished black boots, lowheeled, a white shirt, and black tie, very neat. Sam said to the man who was waiting on him, "I better have some low heels for this fooforaw, hadn't I? Brown'll do."

Fisher said stiffly, "I will see you later, then, sir."

61

"Like you say." Sam turned away, dismissing the man. He knew he had made an enemy and truthfully did not care. The captain had been put down and they both were aware of it. He marched out of the store as if on parade.

Sam found a fine pair of boots, paid his bill, and carried the parcel across to the hotel, wary with every step, knowing that the rats could come creeping out of their holes at the first opportunity. He got to his room without incident, and Dixon brought him warm water. He stripped and washed himself, rubbing his hard body with sensuous enjoyment. He was not one to put on weight, whatever the circumstances, and somehow he was always in top physical condition through no effort on his part. He dried vigorously and dressed with care. He went downstairs and out onto the street, still cautious. There was no one in sight. The City Hall building was brightly lighted and he saw a couple of the blue-shirted men patrolling. This was evidently a special night in Dunstan.

A door was open halfway down the length of the low slung City Hall conglomerate. Before he reached it Sam came to a full stop, listening to music.

It was music the like of which he had once heard in another place. It was slow, waltz time but different. He picked out a horn, the piano keeping the beat, and the strains of a fiddle—but an odd fiddle, dancing the tune, leaving the melody, playing tricks on his ears. The horn soared, then dropped to crooning. He responded to it as he had to Renee's quite different rhythms based on old classics. He wished with all his heart that she was with him to hear.

He leaned against the wall, drinking in the lovely sound. It stopped and he started for the door when it began again. Now it bounced, jumped, still a steady flow but with a different beat. This, suddenly he recognized. His mind went back to a trip he had made to Kansas City.

He had been with boon companions. They were on a toot and had wandered into a high class bordello. There was a band playing. It was composed of blacks, up from New Orleans on the river boats, he had learned. They were playing music very similar to this, though coarser. Still it had been thrilling and he had forgone the whores to listen, drinking beer and chatting with the madame. What had they called it? Jass? Something like that and only the black people could play it. So this was what the Brazile woman had brought with her to charm the wild West.

He entered the room. One of the Olsen twins was on the door, behind a table. Sam said, "Howdy, Sven, how much to enter?"

"You know me already?" He was pleased. "Two dollars to listen. Five to learn the dances."

"I'm more of a listener but here's five in case."

Sven coughed, embarrassed. "Your . . . your gun, Mr. Jones."

"Oh, certain." He unbuckled the belt. "Just keep it handy in case some of these people don't like me."

The boy said seriously, "You betcha, Mr. Jones. And I'll keep an eye open."

"Thanks, friend." Sam had developed a liking for the twins. He saw Oley now, standing with a comely girl. Almost everyone in the room was gathered around a slightly raised dais upon which the musicians were situated.

He could see them plainly, the horn player, the man at the piano and the violinist. They were neither young nor old, it appeared. They wore identical black linsey woolsey coats and pants, not well fitted; pink shirts, string ties, and loose trousers to match the jackets. They were clean shaven—and somehow or other Sam felt that they were lost. They looked, not stared, into the middle distance, as though not aware of the couples and the woman who stood with her back to them and addressed the gathering. There were not more than fifteen couples, Sam saw. All were dressed in the best of western fashions, the women with fresh hairdos, the men wearing jackets. They listened with respect. Several males of varying age were without escorts—the sad imbalance of the West still held, especially in rough new towns like Dunstan. Always there were not enough women to go around.

He spotted young Dunstan, his right hand bandaged, pawing a tall red-haired girl who slapped at him and shoved him away. Cy Dunstan and his wife were in the foreground.

Vera Brazile said, "You are doing well. I know this music and the beat are different from anything you ever heard, but you have the satisfaction of knowing you are the first in the West to hear it, to respond to it. Now we will have another waltz, this one a bit faster. Remember to pivot. The pivot is the soul of the swift waltz, the height of gracefulness."

Sam had edged near to the musicians. Vera Brazile saw him, and as the little band began to play she made her way swiftly to him.

"Mr. Jones. Are you here to listen? Or to learn?"

"Whatever."

"Indeed." She dimpled at him. She was flirting while Dunstan's best people watched. He caught a glimpse of Fisher out of the corner of his eye and saw him flinch.

"Always willin' to learn," Sam said.

She lifted a slim hand to the black men and they began to play Swanee River with a lilting bounce. She held out her arms and said, "Nice and easy at first, please."

Sam said, "Always." He held her firmly a few inches away and began to waltz. The Dunstan people, all eyes, gave way.

Miss Brazile said, "My goodness, gracious. What have we here?"

Sam said, "Dancin's my life."

"I should say so." She was truly graceful, light as a feather. He pivoted once, twice, three times. Then he bent her over in a dip and heard her gasp as his knee went in between her legs. Straightening, he did glide steps almost the length of the floor. The others were barely moving or not moving at all, agape at the exhibition. He went into the reverse pivot that Renee had patiently taught him and the woman spoke again.

"They said you are a gunfighter."

"Dancin' goes with gunfights," he said. "Got to be quick on your feet, y'see?"

"I see a lot." She was slightly out of breath. "I see a man of many parts."

"I see the best dancer I've ever met," he told her.

As they came abreast of the tiny bandstand he saw that the piano player was grinning at him, nodding. He winked and slowed the pace, asking, "Those musicians. Where'd you get 'em?"

There was just a tiny hesitation before she replied, "Why, New Orleans, of course. That's where it begins, the music of the black men, the Creoles—from Africa for all I know. It is so exciting—and I've taught them to play for me."

"You did good." They were making a turn at the corner of the floor when he saw the fancy boot extended in their path. He sidestepped, whirling the lady, then came back stamping hard.

The young Dunstan let out a howl of

pain. The dancers hesitated, stopped. The music went on. Vera Brazile said in a suddenly hard voice, "Go on. Dance. Daniel has been impolite again, that's all."

The red-haired girl who had been partnered with the Dunstan boy said plainly, "He tried to trip Mr. Jones."

Mayor Dunstan lumbered five surprisingly quick steps. He swung a heavy arm, backhanding his son across the face. He said for all to hear, "Git home, you fool. I had enough of you lately."

Mrs. Dunstan pattered over to her boy, clasped his arm, and cried, "You come with me, honey baby. I'll take care of you if your father won't."

Kid Dunstan was led out of the hall holding his twice-damaged jaw. A slight titter rent the air. Captain Fisher stared coldly at the offenders but did not follow the departing pair.

Vera Brazile said to Sam, "Excuse me. I must take over now. You have to keep a strong hand on these folk."

"If anyone can do it, you sure can," he told her.

"Now, folks, please." There was a sharp, commanding undertone in her voice. She could handle these people all right, he thought. The chatter ceased. She lined them up as though they were rookies in a frontier fort.

Sam edged toward the musicians, who waited, straight faced, like black statues. He said, "That's great music."

The did not speak. Their attention was full upon Vera Brazile, he recognized. He said, "Hey, I like it a heap."

Still there was no response. The thin, red-haired girl who had been paired with the Dunstan boy slid away from an expectant partner and came to Sam's side. She said, "They don't talk to nobody. She's got them and everybody else buffaloed."

"Buffaloed?"

"Right. My pappy owns the hotel. You better get outa town tonight, Sam Jones."

"You reckon?"

70

"We like your style. Sven and Oley, too."

"Glad to hear that. What seems to be the danger?"

"If you don't know that you ain't Cemetery Jones," she said flatly. She went across the floor and lined up with Oley Olsen.

Sam saw that Sven Olsen was closing the accounts for the night and joined him. He asked, "Who's the gal with the carrot top?"

"That's Cassie Dixon. From the hotel. She's okay."

"It figures. You know anything I don't?"

"I heard a thing or two. Best you should vamoose quick as you can." Sven spoke in an undertone. Couples were lining up, and Vera Brazile was in full charge as the music began again, a lively beat to distract the gathering from the fracas begun by the mayor's offspring. "The Kid's been shootin' off his mouth. His mama can't hold him down."

"Does he hang out with that bunch of trash in the streets?"

"Well . . . he's got a woman he sees." Sven was uncomfortable. "You know how it is. We don't mess with nice gals."

"I see." The old customs held, even in Dunstan. "Thanks, Sven. I appreciate it."

"We might could help you get outa town."

"Damn decent of you." Sam grinned. "Always been able to manage my own self."

They parted, Sven going to his brother, claiming the red-haired girl for his chance at a dancing lesson. Sam went back to the bandstand. The music fascinated him. He tried to fit his private little tune to the rhythm, "A man can kill another man—and still be on the level—but woe and shame will come to him—who sells out to the devil." It worked if he listened very closely. It flitted across his mind that one of those he had cut down in defense that night might die of infection. He might

72

never know. It was best he did not ever find out.

He watched the dancers. Mayor Dunstan, like so many big, heavy men, was light on his feet, almost graceful. Cap Fisher was stiff as a board. The red-haired Cassie was probably the best of them all, moving with sinewy certainty. Sven was clumsy but earnest. All in all the people of the town were doing well, Sam thought. Now the notion of a cotillion was not farfetched. Vera Brazile was a drill master. He lingered near the music, keeping a low profile. In a short time the musicians began to play "Auld Lang Syne" and the dance lesson was over. Mayor Dunstan spotted Sam and approached him.

"I apologize for that consarned son of mine. Still and all, you spilled a lot of blood around town, Sam Jones."

"Not as much as could be."

"Cap told me. I ain't sayin' it warn't necessary. I'm just sayin' we ain't completely got aholt of things yet. Back-shootin'—you already was bushwhacked once, nearly. Know what I mean?"

"I'll be sayin' adios," Sam said.

"Come again . . . Well, I dunno. You ain't made many friends."

"Time'll tell."

Sam retrieved his gun from Sven, who was in charge of closing up as well. The red-haired Cassie Dixon also lingered. It seemed Oley was to walk her home.

Sam asked, "Where do they keep the musicians?"

"In a rat hole down in the dirty section of town," Cassie said. "They don't get to do anything unless she tells 'em they can, but she feeds 'em good and gives 'em booze."

"Well, they're black, y'see," Oley said defensively. "We only got a couple of black people livin' here. They stay with the Mexes and some drunk Injuns and . . . the rest."

"The nice folks who jumped me?"

"Well . . . yeah."

Sam waited until Sven had locked up, then joined them on the walk to the hotel.

He left them to go into the lobby. Dixon was half asleep behind his desk. Sam asked for his bill, paid it.

"Leavin' early?" asked the hotel man.

"Advised to leave tonight," Sam told him.

"I believe that's smart."

"Could be." He went to his room and packed. He took his gear to the livery stable, roused the owner, and gave him money. He saddled up and rode down the main stem toward Sunrise.

He was glad the night was dark, the moon hidden behind black storm clouds. He came to a copse of trees and pulled off the road. He waited long enough to be satisfied that he was not followed, then turned back. When he came to Dunstan again he rode to the street where the Olsens dwelt. There were no lights on in the house. He tied up to a convenient sapling and walked back to the main street. There were lights only in the section he sought, poverty row. From two saloons and several hovels came noise. There were people suffering from his gunfire hereabouts, he knew. He moved silently and quietly, occasionally looking carefully into windows.

At last he heard the music, muted, coming through a window pasted up with newspapers. He listened to the wail of the trumpet and the soft melancholy sound of the fiddle, feeling that which the black men were telling each other, of their hopelessness not quite complete, of what they longed for but could not demand. When they paused he went to a door through which slits of light shone and knocked, calling, "It's Sam Jones from Sunrise."

There was a long pause. Then a voice asked, "What you want, man from Sunrise?"

"To talk about your music," he said.

The light went out, a bass voice cried, "Go 'way, white man. We don't talk to nobody!"

Immediately a smaller voice whispered, "Walk away, white man. Stop by the tree."

Sam obeyed. There was a lone, skinny

tree a hundred feet away from the hut. He waited. After a few minutes a dark figure sidled up to him and said, "I'se Pompey."

"The piano player," Sam guessed.

"Right." He pronounced it "rat".

"You gave me a sorta sign."

"Had t' grin, you and the boss lady gallivantin'."

"Where you boys from, anyway?"

"New y'Orleans."

"She pick you up there?"

"Uh-uh. River boat. Promised us big money, her did."

"She told me she found you in New Orleans," Sam said.

"She tells lots of folk that."

"How come you're tied up here in this joint?"

"She say no money yet. Later. She say stay down, don't talk to nobody. She say she make us rich," Pompey told him.

"But all she gives you is vittles and booze."

"How you know dat?"

"Someone told me. It's a small town."

Sam listened, thought he heard movement in the pitch dark. He found the elbow of the piano player and led him back the way he had come and around to the other side of the cabin.

The piano player whispered, "You got cat eyes, white man. I never seed a white man with cat eyes befo' now."

"Case of knowin' where you are," Sam told him. "Cap Fisher, now, where's he from?"

"Gawd knows. Army fo' sure. He here befo' we got here."

But not long before, Sam thought. He was trying to piece them together, the two newcomers who had taken over a big part of the town of Dunstan. Again Sam heard a sound in the darkness. He waited, straining his ears. Someone went to the door of the hut and called, "You niggers all tucked in there?"

The bass voice replied, "Yessuh."

Footsteps retreated.

Sam said, "They do that to you every night?"

"Mos' every. She don' want us to git

away. How we gonna do dat is another hoss from a diff'rent stable."

"Where would you go? Best to stick it out awhile," Sam said. He thought of El Sol in Sunrise and how Renee could have a little back-up band and more time to herself—and for him.

"What's to be's to be. We got our music."

"What do you call it—the music?"

"We don' call it nothin'. We just plays it."

"Beautiful."

"It's what we got. Jeb, he blows the horn. Hambone, he fiddles. A banjo, we got it all. Couldn't get Jazzbo, he got knifed."

"You boys carry razors?"

"How do you know that? Don' you tell nobody."

"I've been around," Sam told him. "Keep 'em sharp and maybe somethin' will turn up."

"Any man dance like you been around, all right. That lady, she got this town whoopin'. So she got us. Any time you

79

get idee, we here. We *know* we here." He was neither hopeful nor despairing, Sam realized, he was facing facts and accepting what could not be immediately remedied.

"I'll be goin' along before I get you in trouble. I'll watch you to your door."

Pompey chuckled. "Nobody figures to see me in the dark. Hope t'see you again, Mr. Jones from Sunrise. Love that name for a town—Sunrise."

He was gone without making a sound. Sam waited. The West was not nearly so harsh on black people as other parts of the country, but the line was drawn and Jim Crow persisted in too many ways. He thought about it as he made his way back to where he had left his horse. Black musicians, now, that would be something new in the land.

When he was certain that Pompey had safely entered the hut, he still did not move. The sixth sense that had stood him in good stead on many occasions held him fast. There was someone moving stealthily in the area.

A voice said, "That you Carmody?"

"Yep. Dark as a bull's belly with its tail down."

"Damn niggers. Damn greasers. Damn whores and pimps."

"Cap's right. Keep 'em down. Way down."

These were not the blue clad youths training under Fisher. These were plug uglies. Sam poised, his gun in his hand.

"You see Cap when Cemetery Jones was whirlin' his woman around?"

"She ain't his woman. Yep, I seen him."

"You reckon he ain't got her?"

"Not yet he ain't. Dunstan, maybe. Not Cap."

"Dunstan? The old man?"

"He ain't that old."

"And that wife of his'n, she's a caution. Her and that pulin' brat o' hers."

"Trouble comin' there. What t' hell, we're bein' paid good. Best go on with the rounds."

They parted. One of them stumbled into Sam's arms. He put a hand on the man's shoulder to measure and hit him over the head with the barrel of his gun. He eased him to earth, drew a deep breath and made his way back to the main street. Eavesdropping had gained him little that he did not already know or suspect. It was time to return to Sunrise and make other plans . . . and to watch over Renee.

3

IT was raining in Sunrise, and El Sol was deserted and the bar closed. Upstairs Renee sat with Peggy and Adam Burr. Young Burr had come west the previous year, raw, disowned by his mother, longing to find himself, to learn the true fate of his father. He had succeeded in all this thanks to the help of Sam Jones and others in Sunrise. He had inherited a fortune and entered the banking business with Abe Solomon— and he had married Peggy, the dance hall girl, and built a fine house. He was part of the New West. Renee knew she must confide in him.

She finished her story and added, "We don't want it to get around and upset the town."

"You're right," the young man from Princeton said. "But you must have protection."

She nodded toward the hound lying across the threshold of her door. "It thinks it can take care of that."

Adam knelt and picked up a huge paw. "This hound's been traveling, Renee. It has callouses. The nails are down to the nubs."

"He's hungry, too. Always," she said.

Peggy said, "He looks hungry right now." She took a bonbon from a box on the table and proffered it. It vanished as if by magic.

"One thing about him, he's not choosey," Renee said.

"He's so mournful," Peggy commented.

"His natural expression, I believe," Renee said. "It's always the same, even when he's stuffing himself."

"It's mighty peculiar, the way you described the shooting," Adam said. "As if the dog knew of the danger and meant to warn you."

"I've thought of that. He attached himself to Sam immediately. As if he had a responsibility. You know Sam's not

84

partial to pets. This dog doesn't care. I think he has Sam in his possession."

"True," Adam said. "People don't own certain kinds of dogs. The dogs own them."

Peggy said, "It's too bad about George Spade. It'll be tough to finish the house before winter weather now."

"Not that Sam will be too unhappy." Adam chuckled. "Seems funny that he should own a home, doesn't it? Sam the wanderer."

"It will not prevent him from wandering," Renee said.

"It's in his blood," Adam agreed. "I often wonder whence he came. Who were his parents? How did he come to find gold in this countryside?"

"We'll never know," Peggy said. "He ain't for talkin' about it." Her past was an open book. Orphaned in her teens, she had refused the alternatives of marrying a cowboy, waiting tables, or entering a brothel, and had taken the job of dance girl at El Sol. Not that she hadn't gone upstairs, but at least she'd had her choice of customers under the patronage of Casey Robinson. It was Renee's influence that had kept her wise and independent and ready for the love of a good man.

The rain, which had been pelting against the window, suddenly slackened as it often did on the high plain. Adam picked up their slickers and said, "Time to make a run for it. I hope Sam isn't caught in the storm."

"He won't melt, not our Sam," Peggy said, embracing Renee, donning the slicker. "See you tomorrow."

They were gone, youngsters on the threshold of life. Renee finished her brandy and looked into the mirror on the wall. The tiny lines at the corners of her eyes were deep; she was weary after a long night at the piano. Her worry about Sam, always concealed, also took its toll, she knew. Talk of the past had brought secret thoughts to the surface, memories she wished with all her heart would vanish. It had started deep within her earlier when the young folks naturally and innocently had asked if there was anyone she knew about who would want to kill her.

She had answered the negative, which so far as she knew was true. The one person who might have wanted her dead was himself deceased. There were people who disliked her, a few who probably still thought fondly of her, and one who perhaps still loved her. But there was no one who had a reason to murder.

She undressed slowly. The rain again began to assail the window. She peered from behind the shade at an impenetrable black night. She washed off the minimal rouge and powder that she daily applied with such skill. She went to the closet and took out a black robe with a scarlet lining and wrapped herself in it. She went to her table; opened a drawer and took out an over-and-under-derringer Sam had given her and put it in the pocket of the robe. She was too restless to go to sleep; it was stuffy in the room and she needed to move her body. She went downstairs and through the saloon, smelling the stale smoke of cigars, and to the inner heavy door and opened it and went through the swinging doors to the long veranda.

The fresh wet air was a tonic. A breeze swept little rain devils along the open porch. She welcomed them against her feet and ankles. She walked slowly up and down, trying to throw off the track a train of memories that persisted. There had been her happy childhood, her music always to the fore, Europe during the War Between the States, her early blossoming into a beauty with all the pros and cons of that condition. There had been the man she could not love, a fine man, a powerful man, he who had the best intentions but was not for her. There had been . . . but she determinedly stopped. She simply would not retrace the years of debacle, of flight. She had found a home in the town of Sunrise, in this overpoweringly beautiful country, among good people who accepted her without question. And she had found Samuel Hornblow Jones.

He provided the perfect balance for times like this. His calm, laid back coolness kept her on an even keel. Even he did not know the fires deep beneath her surface, although at times she thought he suspected. He was a tower of strength for her. She turned and walked the other way and then for the first time realized that the awkward hound was with her. He was plodding along, invisible in the dark, making no iota of sound.

She said, "Dog, you are amazing. If tonight there were shadows you would be one of them, wouldn't you?"

The sound of the rain was comforting; the company of the dog was reassuring. She had not thought of the danger, which was extraordinary; she seldom if ever lost a jot of her wits.

The dog suddenly made a sound, a deep one, from his gut. She was at the north end of the veranda of El Sol. She wheeled around and saw a figure leaping toward her. She saw the dull gleam of a knife in the darkness. The dog ran past her and a swinging arm just missed her throat. She put her hand in the cloak pocket and fired without drawing the powerful little gun. She fell back against the wall of El Sol.

The dark figure staggered, groaning, and she took out the derringer and fired again. The man fell and writhed on the walk. The hound jumped upon him. He moved no more. The dog returned and stood at her side, silent. She froze, horrified.

Finally she made her walk indoors and called for Shaky, who slept in a back room. He came with a lantern. He said, "My Gawd in heaven, Miss Renee, what's goin' on?"

"I think we have a dead man outside." She was faint but still in control.

"Did you fire them shots?"

"I did. The dog saved me."

He went out into the night. She made herself follow. The would-be assassin lay on his back. Shaky leaned close and said, "Cactus Joe. A damn bad breed, Miss Renee. Must've wanted to break in and rob. I'll get Donovan."

"Yes. Get the marshal." She was shaking like a leaf in the continuing breeze. The dog was close to her now and she felt its presence and it gave her the strength to sit at a table and wait. Shaky lit a lamp and went, hastily dressed, out into the storm. She walked to the bar and poured a stiff drink of whiskey and returned to her seat. The dog nestled close, nuzzling her. She spoke to it.

"Now we know, don't we? Now we know how Sam feels when he has killed a person. We only guessed at it before."

She shivered and gulped the strong liquor. The doors sprang open and Peggy and Adam came in, stared and rushed to her. "We heard what happened."

She said, "It had to be done. He had a knife. Dog was on him but it had to be done."

Peggy put her arms around her. "Sure it had to be done. We all know that."

"I know the feeling," Adam told her. "I know how it is." It had not been too long since he'd had the same experience, a green kid from the East fighting for the lives of others.

It helped but still there was that

shuddering in her. The whiskey settled her down as time passed, and the marshal came, and then Dr. Bader with his wagon, and the body was carted away and Donkey Donovan was asking her the question that she had been fearing.

"If he was out to rob El Sol how come he jumped you with the knife? It don't make sense, he coulda just waited."

She had her reply ready. "It was pitch dark. The dog went for him. He probably thought I was a man."

Shaky said, "Some dog. Don't look like much but he acts like somethin'."

More people came and marveled and sympathized until she could have screamed. She managed with the help of the whiskey, told and retold the story until she was hoarse. Finally she refused the Burrs' offer to take her home with them and was alone. She found horehound for her throat and bar jerky for Dog and went slowly and painfully up the stairs.

In bed she said, "Dog, you took Sam's

place but oh how I wish he was here right now."

Sleep came through exhaustion, bringing dreams she would far rather not have had.

Sam was wet right through his slicker. He was also dead tired. The rain showed no mercy in the black of the night. He remembered a cabin off the road a couple of hundred yards that he had seen on another occasion. There was a chance he might find it again despite the dark. He turned off the road. A few hours would make little difference. He needed time to sort things out, and he needed sleep.

A dozen rods into the trees and he reined in. There was the sound of horses slopping through the mud of the road. Someone with a loud voice said, "Whoa."

"Yeah. Whoa," said another. "What the hell we doin'? We ain't never gonna catch Jones with a late start in this here weather."

The first man said, "And if we do, someone's goin' to get kilt, believe me."

A third, indecisive, said, "Well . . . we're gettin' paid."

"Nobody payin' us is fool enough to be out in this here black damn weather themselves."

"There's a shanty up the road here a piece," said the loud one. "We could stay awhile and say he got clean away into town."

"Supposin' we got somebody trailin' us?"

There was a silence. Sam turned the black horse into the trees, off the weeded path. He drew his rifle from its scabbard and waited. The first speaker was right on the nose, he thought. If he was seen there would be some shooting.

"I'm for doin' as Babbit says."

"Well . . . I'll hang around and watch the back trail," said a fourth voice.

"Come on, then."

They turned up the path. Sam sat still as a statue. They rode by, three of them. He debated about the lookout, then relaxed. The rain continued to pour down in buckets.

The watcher was evidently no more comfortable. He rode past Sam and on the trail of his companions.

Now there was a choice. Should Sam follow and try to learn something that would help his quest for whoever was out to kill Renee? Or should he be glad of his luck and ride for home? There were several old sayings to mull over in his mind: "Better safe than sorry."

"Let well enough alone."

"Nothing ventured, nothing gained."

A rusty, cracked voice said behind him, "Look before you leap, friend."

Sam said, "I've got to believe you have the drop on me."

"Nope."

"Why not?"

"'Cause you ain't with them jaspers ridin' ahead."

"You know something I oughta know?"

"Mebbe. Mebbe not. You the feller they calls Cemetery Jones, aincha?"

"Could be."

"I 'spect you know them bastids is after you."

"How do you know that?" Sam asked.

"I been in that burg back yonder."

"You got a name?"

"People calls me Beaver." He chuckled. "Trapped a few in my day. 'Course that's quite a ways back."

"Beaver McLaine?"

"You heard o' me?"

Sam had thought the old mountain man dead years ago. He said, "Why, sure. You're about the last of 'em."

"Jest about." Again the rattling chuckle. "Got somethin' to do afore I check out."

"I've got somethin' to do right now, seems like. If you're of a mind to go along."

"If it's a mischief agin those bastids mought be I'd enjoy it."

A blast of thunder came and a shaft of lightning bathed the old man. Sam's quick eye picked up the picture; bent, broad shoulders, beaver hat, buckskins, a beard. More than any men, Sam admired

96

these conquerors of the Old West, these men who had walked mountains carrying their possibles on their backs, made friends with Indians, killed Indians, slept with squaws, trapped beaver, and sold it in Taos where they spent the gains on more supplies and much raw liquor only to return to the wilderness. They had discovered the West, and some of them had settled in it. Kit Carson had fought in the War. Jim Bridger had built a fort. Jed Smith had opened California. And on and on, Sam knew all the tales. Here was one of those heroes.

Beaver said, "These bastids is hired guns, you know that?"

"I didn't reckon they were Cap Fisher's raw kids."

"Fisher, he's the one. Pays good for the bastids."

"Think we better go afoot?"

"Yaas indeedy."

"My horse is hired."

Beaver chuckled. "You leave him with ol' Mossy and he won't stir a foot."

Old Mossy was a tall mule. Sam had

heard of the mountain man's preference for the tough hybrids. He dismounted. He said, "Long guns won't be necessary, right?"

"Sartain. Do we go straight ahead?"

"Right up this path if it's the right one. Which I now believe it to be."

There was another saying in his head which seemed to be full of them this stormy night: "Never judge a man 'til you've walked a mile in his footsteps." He could never judge Beaver, therefore he led the way himself, and not without some trepidation. He had learned the Indian way of moving without sound but men like Beaver had lived it.

He felt that Beaver was walking in his footsteps, all right, and tried to remember approximately how far the shack had been from the road. It was now certain that the horsemen had found it, otherwise they would be on their way back. If he was wrong there would indeed be a fracas, four against two and he did not know what the mountain man was carrying.

Probably a Bowie rather than a pistol, he thought; they rarely carried short guns.

The storm pelted them but Sam was so wet that it no longer mattered. His eyes were beginning to be accustomed to the darkness, for which he was grateful. He figured the cabin was about two hundred yards up the path and counted his footsteps. He had been right; he saw the bulk of the small, battered building where he had remembered it, two hundred paces, a bit more. He stopped and whispered in Beaver's ear.

"I can't shoot 'em down cold. The horses?"

"Keerect. The hosses." Beaver slipped ahead of him.

Sam followed. They came closer to the shack. There was no light but they could hear voices and the gurgle of a bottle being passed around. They crouched, all ears for that moment.

Babbit, the loudmouth, was speaking. "Four like us'ns to get one man. I know he's bad but nobody's that bad."

Someone said in reply, "How many did he down, anyways?"

A third spoke up. "Mebbe fifty. Why d'you think they call him 'Cemetery'?"

The fourth man chimed in. "Up in Dodge he kilt Doby Simms. Youall mind Doby?"

"Fast man."

"Friend o' mine. Jones got him with his gun half drew and turned on me so fast I swallowed m' chaw. Now that's fast."

"You seen him work, then?"

"One time and that was plenty."

Babbit asked, "How come Cap knows about him? Cap's a damn tenderfoot."

"Gawd knows. Cap's an ornery one."

"Where's he gettin' his money?"

"He ain't talkin'."

Babbit's voice rode high. "You c'n talk about how fast Jones is. But I seen Cap Fisher teachin' them young uns to draw and I'm tellin' the world—he's lightnin'."

"Then why ain't *he* out here lookin' for Jones?"

"Mebbe 'cause he can pay suckers like us to do the job."

"Four of us."

"Ain't no man in the world can stop us four."

The bottle gurgled again, four times. Babbit said, "Hell, let's get some shut eye if we can. I'm so damn wet it don't make no never mind, now."

Beaver touched Sam's arm, drawing away. Sam followed him. They came to where the four riders had made a cavayar for the horses with a length of rope. Beaver produced a Bowie knife and sliced the rope, cooing to the horses a soft tune, almost indistinguishable to Sam, who was at his side. The animals followed the mountain man down the road. Sam was the rear guard, Colt drawn. Beaver handled the horses so that they made no sound save the sucking noise of their hoofs in the mud.

Down the path a hundred paces Beaver stopped and said, "Reckon I've spilt more liquor than most folks drink. It does

101

muddle the head. While they're sleepin' it off, we got what they need."

Sam, teeth chattering, said, "I'd admire to have a sip of muddle-head stuff right now."

They came to where their mounts stood side by side, heads down, mournful in the downpour. They mounted up and Sam said, "You sure got a way with horses. Reckon we better take these four along?"

"Chances be their brands is marked over more'n once. Why not take 'em into town?"

"You got good notions. And when we hit the road I got some muddleness in my saddlebag."

"Waugh!" Beaver said. It was the gutteral sign of the mountain man that he was highly pleased.

They went slowly and carefully to the main road. Beaver spoke to the horses and they actually whinnied in their misery. Sam marveled. When they had organized the drive he took a bottle of whiskey from his saddlebag and extended it to Beaver, who despite the dark of the night, found it with ease. Each drank deeply and sighed in partial relief as they bent their way toward Sunrise and shelter from the elements.

Sam ran over in his mind what he had overheard. Only one positive fact had been substantiated: Captain Steve Fisher wanted him dead.

Now it needed to be learned if his death related to the shots fired at Renee. There could only be one conclusion. Since Sam stood in the way of Renee's murder, Fisher was connected to the failed bush-whacking. This led him to the dog, which had come from Dunstan to Sunrise.

He was a man who kept to himself, who spoke only when necessary, yet in the dark and the rain, plodding along in the mud he found himself talking aloud to his new acquaintance. "We were settin' on the stoop, the lady and me, and this dog comes along and we lean over and some jasper shoots at the lady and because of the dog he misses. I go after him and he don't even try to pick me off. He's gone. But now this here Fisher is tryin' to have me killed. Only thing I come up with is he didn't know who I was, didn't give a damn about me at that time, only wanted to kill her. She don't know why. The dog, it's a kinda loco animal that adopts me. It eats like four hogs. There's a connection some place because it came from Dunstan to Sunrise. None of this makes any real sense, y'see?"

The rain pelted them. Beaver said, "Had a dog once up no'th in high country. Starvin' we was. Got track of a deer; he was a tracker. He stopped, wouldn't move an inch. Couldn't get past him. Heard a howl. Creeped up. There was a grizzly, had the deer. Woulda got me sure. Shot the bear, the deer was dead already. Waugh. We et off 'em for weeks."

"Man's best friend. I never owned one before. Seems like I got one now. If he could talk I'd bet he could tell what's happenin'," Sam said. "That bush-whacker now, it could be he didn't have the sand to risk missin' me and took off."

"Bushwhackers tend to be smart enough to know to get you and then go in after the lady. It's a puzzlement, that part."

"It don't make sense," Sam said.

"Plenty things that don't make sense happen alla time," Beaver said. "It's a worry, though. Patience won't cut it."

"Patience gets you killed," agreed Sam.

He became silent with his thoughts. They rode on and came to the outskirts of Sunrise at dawn and drove the horses to where Adam Burr had his ranch outside town, put them in the corral without awakening anyone, then rode back into Main Street and to the livery stable.

Sam said, "We can put up here, then go to the hotel. There's a room next to mine. They know me good, it won't be a bother to anybody."

"Waugh," Beaver said. "Jest so I can rinse out."

In the light of a lamp he was taller than Sam had judged, hairy to his shoulders, sharp-nosed, with large, bright blue eyes.

He wore moccasins and fringed leg gins with his buckskins and carried a leather pouch swung over his shoulder. He looked around the comfortable room Sam opened for him and nodded, twinkling. "Ain't seen anything like this in a space o'time. Sleep well, Sam Jones; sleep well."

"You too. And thanks."

Sam was undressed in a jiffy, dried and clothed in dry garments. He heard the mountain man snoring as he crept from the hotel in his slicker and ran down to El Sol. As he knew she would be, Renee was waiting for him.

4

THE storm ceased mid-afternoon, but the skies remained sulky. In Dunstan there was little movement on Dunstan Avenue. The false-front buildings dripped in forlorn silence. The saloons were full of somnolent clients.

At Mayor Dunstan's house Vera Brazile presided over tea, with Mrs. Dunstan and Captain Fisher in attendance. On a fair day there would have been other ladies; it was part and parcel of the package of elegance the dancing lady had brought to town.

She said brightly, "It was a good meeting in spite of everything, was it not?"

"Not when my boy was hurt," Mrs. Dunstan said, her eyes red from weeping. "Cyrus is just too mean, damn him."

"The boy needs discipline," Fisher said

mildly. "I will point out the problems to him. He'll be fine."

"We all depend on you for so much," Vera Brazile said.

"Matter of duty. The mayor has given me leeway to keep the boy on the narrow path."

"Danny's not one to follow no narrow path," cried his mother. "He's a real westerner. He goes his own way. He's strong and a leetle too fond of fun. Be nice to him, you hear, Cap?"

"Certainly." There was reservation in his agreement and they both felt it.

Vera Brazile said softly, "Oh, I think Captain Fisher will not be too harsh. Will you, sir?"

"Of course not." He looked directly at her. "Just some hard work which never hurt anybody—and a talk, advice, that is."

There was a knock at the door. Fisher answered. Before him stood Babbit, mud covered, shoulders slumped. Behind Babbit were the three who had ridden out with him, all in the same woebegone condition.

Fisher said harshly, "You failed."

"Injuns," lied Babbit. "We got bush-whacked. They stole our hosses and our guns."

"And why didn't they kill you?"

Babbit took off his hat, displaying a self inflicted round hole in the felt. "Come near to it. Reckon they didn't want that much on their heads when they git rounded up. Stealin's one thing. Killin's another."

"This is the first I heard that the Apaches were out," Fisher said. "What about Jones?"

"He had a start. Must've got to Sunrise."

Fisher debated a moment, then said, "Out to the ranch."

"Jeez, Cap, we ain't cowpokes. We got no guns and we're busted."

"You take the hay wagon and get to the ranch. That's an order. You get no pay for work unfinished. Remember that."

Babbit said, "But we're cold. We ain't

et nothin'; we need a drink real bad."

Fisher stared at him without replying. After a moment Babbit turned and the others turned with him. Fisher went back into the house.

The red-haired girl walked from the hotel to the butcher shop, picking her way in short boots. Oley was helping the hired butcher, whose name was Pate. The young man wiped his hands on a bloodied apron and said, "Hi, Cassie. You come for the order?"

"Yeah," she said, showing no haste, leaning against the counter. She was long-legged and straight-backed and slightly freckled and almost pretty. Her green eyes were her best feature; they were sharp. "You made up to that Jones fella, didn't you?"

"You had an eye on him yourself, didn't you?" Oley said.

"The Kid was pawin' me all evening. I liked it when Jones stomped him."

"That was plenty good."

"You want to help me with the order?"

110

"Sure. Pate, I'll be right back."

"If you ain't you send for Sven, you hear?" the butcher said.

They gathered the packages of meat for the hotel, divided them up, and started down the street. Cassie moved like a colt avoiding the puddles, a thoroughbred filly, he thought. He wanted to marry her but everyone said they were too young.

They put the meat in the large hotel refrigerator and looked at one another. Oley said softly, "Sven is with Cap Fisher in the big hall. A lecture."

"On killin' people," she said. She led the way down the side street to the Olsen house. They went into the parlor and sat on a couch and embraced. They kissed long and ardently, but when his hand strayed she put it aside, saying, "Now, darlin'." He desisted, sighing but amenable.

She went on, "I saw something last night. Couldn't sleep. You know my room, upstairs, on the street?"

"How could you see anything? It was pitch black."

"Just shapes. And voices. You know that big fella named Babbit? Him and two or three other rannies rode out toward Sunrise."

"Babbit's Cap's man. A no-good."

"Well, they came back a while ago. Walkin'. No guns."

"You saw that?" Oley asked.

"Just happened to. You reckon they were after Jones?"

"I knew Jones was goin' to leave. It could be. I'll bet he outsmarted 'em somehow or other," Oley said.

"Do you think they were after him on account of him takin' care of the Kid in Sunrise and at the dance?"

He said, "I don't think the mayor is up to that. He'd rather show off and have it peaceful."

"Cap's always suckin' up to him. What if old Dunstan didn't know about it?"

"Could be." Oley frowned and said, "Best keep this to ourselves, Cassie."

"And Sven." She knew he could never keep anything from his twin brother; it was part of their existence. She went on,

"Reckon we don't have to go and tell Jones about it. Reckon he knows."

"Just if he comes back here."

"Yes. If he comes back here."

He kissed her and said, "I got to get back to the shop or Pate'll have a fit. I do love you, Cassie."

She put her long arms around him and whispered, "They better let us get married soon. Damn Swedes got to marry late, your papa always says. I don't want to wait any more'n you do."

He released her, then hugged her again. "I don't feel like no Swede around you."

"More like a goat," she said, pushing him away.

They parted with decorum and Cassie went back to the hotel. Her father, a worried, balding man, was behind the desk.

She said, "Pa, why do we stay here in this lousy town?"

"Because Cyrus Dunstan's got a mortgage on us and folks ain't crazy about stoppin' off here."

"He's got a mortgage on the town."

113

"That's right. We got to put another couple tables in the dining room. People are beginnin' to eat here. Josie's good in the kitchen."

"More work for me." But Cassie smiled and patted his shoulder.

"If you married Oley we might could get cheaper prices on the meat." He was only half joking.

"The Olsens say we're too young."

"I was your age when I married your ma. And they weren't much older. Folks is strange sometimes."

"If we only had a man like Sam Jones in town."

"And six or seven others of 'em." Oliver Dixon returned to his books.

She went into the kitchen where Josie, a gaunt Yankee widow, was preparing for dinnertime. Despite her outward bold bearing, Cassie had doubts of the future in Dunstan.

Cyrus Dunstan drove the carriage past his acreage, past herds of wet, downcast cattle, up the circular driveway to his hacienda. The D Bar D was a showplace, everything in order, staffed with workers, a cook, a housekeeper, a teenage boy for the chores, a hay barn, a horse stable, cowboys a-plenty, and a house built of hard wood large enough to accommodate a dozen guests. He ceremoniously handed down Vera Brazile and his wife.

"Here we are. Doggone rain, watch your step. You gals get ready for a big ol' meal."

"How nice of you," Vera Brazile said. "What a lovely house."

Liz Dunstan said, "We bought all the furniture in El Paso. Wait'll you see."

They tripped through puddles and went indoors. Cy Dunstan went to the bunkhouse seeking his segundo. He found him braiding a rope, a burly man named Tom Vaughn. Sitting on four of the many bunks were Babbit and his cohorts in sin.

Dunstan said, "Tom."

"Yessir." He had a bass voice. "These came in on the supply wagon."

"No horses?"

Babbit said, "Apaches got us."

"Where the hell were you in the rain that Injuns could git you?"

"Cap Fisher sent us out," Babbit said.

"For what damn reason?"

"Well, he wanted to make sure that Cemetery Jones'd left town."

"So you trailed him?"

"Until the Injuns ambushed us."

"How come they didn't ambush Jones?"

Babbit shrugged.

Vaughn said, "Mebbe they knowed him."

"You know him?" Dunstan asked.

"I been around a while. Met him in Abilene. He killed Obie Dailey there. Fastest man I ever seen."

"People keep tellin' me that. Seemed a quiet sort to me."

"He ain't a gunner," Vaughn said. He jerked a thumb toward Babbit and the others. "Not like these."

Dunstan said, "So Cap sent you out here. We don't need help out here."

"They can swamp the stable and barn,"

Vaughn said indifferently. "Let some real cowmen loose. If there's Apaches out we'll need 'em with the herd."

"We ain't no swampers," bellowed Babbit.

"You're hired hands." Dunstan could talk louder than the discomfited gunman. "Cap sent you out here. You wanta quit?"

They were broke and without horses. Babbit opened his mouth, shut it.

Vaughn said, "You can go to work right now. The kid that does the chores'll show you what needs doin'."

They left. Vaughn shook his head.

"I ain't for havin' their kind around."

"Cap hired 'em. Reckon he's punishin' them for missin' out on his orders. You know how he is."

"Long as he don't order me."

"He won't. He's town. You're boss here," Dunstan said.

Vaughn said, "Things are smooth enough here. You believe it about Apaches?"

"I wouldn't believe Babbit on a stack o' Bibles. Best to set a watch, though."

117

"Consider it set."

"You're a good man, Tom. No problems?"

"None."

"Got to get you into town for the dance. Big doin's."

"Not for me," the foreman said. "Got two left feet."

Dunstan sat down at the long table in the center of the wide room. "Set yourself, Tom."

Vaughn sat opposite him. Dunstan took a flask from his pocket and passed it. "Best whiskey in the territory. About Babbit and them. We was both in the War, right?"

"I got the scars to prove it."

"If us Rebs was allowed to fight 'em even with cornstalks we'd of won. But they had more guns and more men."

"Them kids from Ohio and Minnesota sure could stand up," Vaughn said.

"You mind Vicksburg?"

"Gen'ral Grant killed thousands of them kids."

"And took the Mississippi. And Sherman?"

"He wasted Georgia and cut us in half."

"Grant and Sherman, they didn't worry how many they kilt."

"Won the damn war."

"So I put up with Babbit. I don't even know the names of t'other three. Don't give a damn. I got a job to do cleanin' up the town. I need Cap Fisher to do it," Dunstan said.

"You certain that's the way?"

"It's the only way. It's my way. You been with me long enough to know."

"I been with you since you started with the cows."

Dunstan grinned. "Swung a wide loop, didn't we?"

"Who didn't?"

"That ain't the way I got my start." Dunstan picked up the flask and took a long swig. "Fella found traces of gold over in Arizona. Got drunk and bragged on it. I filed a claim. He come at me and I shot him. All legal. But I had to be ready with the gun, I had to think ahead of him. And several others."

"You always been square with me."

"You're my top man. The only one I trust. Now about that son o' mine."

Vaughn shook his head. "Roarin' down the pathway t'hell."

"I took his mother out of a whorehouse. Hell, there wasn't much choice in them days if you didn't have the dinero. She's been a good wife. Plenty others I knowed did the same. It's just she's loco about Danny."

"Give him to me."

"Can't do it. She'd cry tears enough for a river. Wish I could give her another baby. Can't seem to. Now there's the Brazile woman."

"Where'd she come from?"

Dunstan said soberly, "She come with a letter from one of the biggest wigs in New York City. She's got money, too. Says she's got a mission. Civilize the West. Well, that's just what the town needs. It's kinda fun."

"Dancin' around a hard floor ain't my kinda fun."

"It keeps people happy. You know what I did? I sent notices to the newspapers in El Paso, Denver, San Francisco, wherever there's folks wantin' to move. Come to Dunstan, you're all welcome."

Vaughn stared, then laughed. "Cy, you're goin' to get some fancy dudes all right. Every crook with an itch to travel."

"That's why I got Cap Fisher and such as Babbit."

"Just you keep that Fisher away from me. I got a feelin' about him."

"He keeps the young uns in line and serves to maintain the law. My law. He may be a stiff joint but he's my stiff joint," Dunstan said.

"He's trouble."

"What ain't? I come here, settle a town, take a look at what's been done up in Sunrise. I'm late. I get the leavin's. So I work on it. One day Dunstan'll be bigger and more important than Sunrise, you mark my words."

121

"What good'll that do you? Way it is, you own everything in sight, you got your woman, you got your health."

"It ain't enough." Dunstan grinned suddenly. "Nothin' ain't never enough. Now you wash up and come in to dinner."

He pocketed the flask, slapped Vaughn on his thick shoulder and went to the house.

Vera Brazile was saying, "I understand Mr. Jones has a lady friend."

"Humph. Plays pianna in a saloon," Liz Dunstan said. "Puts on airs. Wears dresses like . . . like yours."

"It's a high-class saloon," Cy Dunstan said. "I'm goin' to spruce up a joint after the next shipment of ore from Tombstone. Got a mine over there," he explained to Vera Brazile. "Made my first strike thereabouts."

"You do have varied interests," she said admiringly. "You are one of the western barons, Mister Mayor."

"You got to learn to call me 'Cy'

y'know. Got to be a bit western yourself now you're here."

"Very well, Cy." She laughed merrily. "I declare this country becomes more enchanting all the time. Captain Fisher was saying the same thing the other day."

"I ain't too keen on Fisher," Liz Dunstan said. "He's too hard on my boy."

"Now, now. Daniel will grow up. He's just going through his salad years," Vera Brazile said.

"Salad years?" Liz Dunstan was puzzled.

"Youth must be served." Vera Brazile did not alter her smile.

"He'll be served up like a trussed turkey iffen he don't mind his ways," Cyrus Dunstan said.

"Vera knows what she's talkin' about," his wife said. "You was a wild boy yourself."

"I was workin' down in a mine at his age. I'd been workin' my—uh—my tail off for eight years and more by that time."

"Now don't start that. . . ."

The evening wore on. Dinner was announced and Tom Vaughn came in and was introduced and unimpressed by the eastern lady, even while she flirted with him over the table laden with quail, beef, four kinds of vegetables, and bottles of red wine.

Captain Stephen Fisher was established in an adobe house on the far edge of town, away from the riff raff. He had a Mexican boy come in to clean up—he was not a man to have women about if it could be prevented. He ate his meals in the hotel and had his washing done by the Chinese laundry. He rode a fine chestnut stallion to and fro in town, sitting tall in the saddle, a proper military figure.

Right now he was having supper in the Dixon hotel. Across from him was Kid Dunstan, who was having trouble with his utensils because of his bandaged hand and was otherwise out of sorts, glum, monosyllabic.

Fisher said, "One thing you must

always remember, never overmatch yourself. You did it in Sunrise, then you failed to learn a lesson, and you did it again here. Cemetery Jones is not a man to trifle with."

"I know." Then the kid blurted, "If I get him without his gun I'll make ploughlines of his guts."

"You'll never get the chance. And if you did it wouldn't work. He's too quick for you. I've told you over and over to work on your speed. You're too lazy, Daniel. I'm warning you now. You're going to work your tail off this week."

"I don't have to. My pa owns this burg."

"Your father will not give you any more money until you show him you'll work hard. Your mother will only have enough to run the homes."

"My ma will . . ."

"Those are the new orders," Fisher said crisply. "You will attend our meetings. Or you will work at the ranch. And I intend to take to the field for maneuvers at once. Get that in your head."

"Hell."

"It will be close to that." Fisher paid his share of the bill to Dixon. Cassie refused to wait on Kid Dunstan, he knew. That he considered none of his business. He also knew that young Dunstan would be going to a whore tonight—his credit would be good in that part of town.

He said, "You mark my words, young fellow, and toe the mark or you will be in deep trouble."

He left and rode back to his house. He put up his horse with great care. He entered the kitchen and saw that the boy had everything in order, exactly as he had given instructions. He went into the parlor and sat in a straight chair and picked up a history of Texas, by one H. Yoakum, published in 1855, one of two dull, lengthy volumes which he had found in El Paso. After a few minutes he put it down. He went into his bedroom and closed the blinds against the insistent, driving rain. There was, oddly, a pier glass mirror in a corner. Mechanically, he donned his cartridge belt. He stood in front of the glass and began practising the fast draw with his .38 calibre Smith & Wesson.

That was the way it had all begun. He had been a yearling at West Point. An upperclassman had accused him of cheating on a history examination. He had called the man out and because he was deft had shot him. He had been dismissed. His father had disowned him.

He'd changed his name before he wandered to Kansas. He had killed a man over a card game—again the cheating. He did not understand it; he knew that others cheated and were never caught. It was his luck, he believed. Until now his luck had always, in the end, deserted him. Now, with his name again altered, he had another chance.

The mayor was smart. He paid good money and he expected results. There was no reason to be anything but honest with him. The woman, now, was another matter.

He was sweating from his exertions as he moved faster and faster. The picture of Sam Jones was somewhere on the edge of his mind. One bit of bad luck and he would have to face Jones; he was dead certain of that.

The damn kids were easy. He could use his West Point training on them. Dunstan gave him the authority, and the tradition of the West gave him solidarity in their minds—be ready, be strong, be brave.

The cloud in his head remained. He would, he swore, not let it dismay him. He had an opportunity to move into a position of power. That was all he had ever needed, power. The good life would follow. He must believe his luck would change—had changed. He made three swift draws and his arm ached and he quit. He had no real fear of facing Jones. It was all a matter of circumstances.

He went into the kitchen where the boy always left a tin tub half-full of cold water. He stripped to sponge himself, a strict discipline. He scowled at the tooth marks on his legs where the damned, mangy dog had bitten him. The miserable hound had interrupted him, begging for food, as he was en route to the stable, and he had kicked at it. Amazing how quick the ugly animal had been, he thought, and how it had vanished before he could recover and draw his revolver.

He sought his Spartan bed. Tomorrow he would take the boys into the field, the wet, muddy field, and teach them what he had learned at the Point. He was building an army for Mayor Cyrus Dunstan—and himself. With an army, a disciplined band of men, he would have power. Meantime there was the other job to be done. . . .

5

IT was another evening in El Sol. Sam was trying to convey to Renee the rhythm of the black men in Dunstan. She understood, but when she tried to play the piano in that mood it was not quite right.

"It's like their—uh—souls are in it." He was surprised at his attempt to explain it in those words. "I dunno. Like a hymn, but not like a hymn."

"I've read about them," she said. "An African influence, the man wrote. I'd love to hear them." She was wan and weary. They had talked and he had related to her the many sins of Cactus Joe and how every decent person wanted him dead, but he had known it did not help. She had taken the life of a human being. That he indeed knew all about.

He said, "There's a few people down there don't like me too much. Maybe we'll get to hear the black men one way or t'other, though. I sure want us to."

The dog lay between them at their special table in the rear of the saloon. It was a dull night to match the dull weather after the storm. The poker game was notable for its rare absence. Mayor Wagner and Frank Wilson of the general store were missing. Donkey Donovan came in and wiped his brow as he sat down with Renee and Sam.

"That mountain man of your is some kinda punkin," he said.

"He is, he is," Sam agreed.

"First the barber shop. Said he was wet clean through and just needed some soap lather. Got his beard shaved, you wouldn't know him." Donkey paused, frowned and added, "There's somethin' familiar about him, though. Like I knowed him before."

"Sam says he's looking for his granddaughter," said Renee.

"Yeah, huh? Well, he's buyin' at the store. I mean, he's buyin' city clothes. Said he'd meet us here. Said his granddaughter was white. Never did marry a squaw in church, just Injun ways. Said he heard his son got killed by Apaches." Donkey spoke slower and slower. "Said he made a strike and was lookin' to spend it on the gal."

Sam blinked and said, "I'll be a monkey's uncle."

Before any more could be ventured the swinging doors flew open with a bang and Beaver McLaine stood in all his glory bellowing, "Whereat's my friend Sam Jones?"

He wore a purple and bright green shirt, striped gambler's pants, a yellowish leather belt from which dangled a lanyard holding a long, sharp skinning knife, and his worn moccasins. On his head was a flat-brimmed Mexican-style hat.

Sam rose and announced to all present, "This here is Beaver McLaine, last of the mountain men. He'll do to cross any river with."

"Waugh. Drinks are on me. Belly up, folks."

Beaver tossed a gold piece on the bar

and pigeon-toed his way to the table. The light fell full upon his face as he removed his hat and dropped it on the floor. His cheeks were pink from their first shave in many a year. His features were surprisingly delicate; when he smiled his teeth were white and even. His long nose was thin. His bright blue eyes were those of a far younger man.

Sam said under his breath, "I'll be damned."

Renee touched his hand and nodded. "Me too."

Beaver was orating, "They do have the fine duds nowadays. Always did like color, bright color. Couldn't wear the boots, though. Been too long without crammin' my feet into 'em. Nice feller at the store. Said he knew you good, Sam. Reckon everybody and his brother around here knows you good."

Sam said, "Got some friends here."

The blue eyes fixed on the marshal. "This here lawman's been starin' at me like I was wanted. Sonny, it's been many a year since I broke a law." He laughed deep in his chest and turned to Renee. "Little lady I heered about what happened to you. Don't let it rankle. It's bad for you, I know that all righty. But let it go away. Time cures. You did right. Let it pass."

She replied, "Thank you, Beaver."

"Kilt my first man when I was fifteen," he said. "I was with Carson in Taos, just come from Virginny. Fella was drunk and come at me with a club. They was a big hiyu goin' on, whiskey flowin'. I didn't know nothin' excepting that when you git in a tight spot you got to move."

Shaky came with a tray of drinks. He too took a long look, then said, "Howdy, Mr. McLaine."

"Don't you mister me, friend. Beaver, that's me. Ev'body knows me calls me Beaver." He held up his glass, drained it, handed it back. "Waugh! Good liquor. I'll take one more."

Shaky returned with a bottle of Monongahela rye and said, "My feet's too sore to be runnin'. He'p yourselves."

Casey Robinson came from his office in

the rear, leaned over to Renee and said, "It's so slow tonight. Why don't you take off, darlin'?"

She said, "That is not why I'm here, thank you, my dear."

She went to the piano and played "Buffalo Gals," and the conversation at the bar lightened. A cowboy danced with one of the girls. Beaver jumped to his feet, howling "Waugh!" and began to show Sunrise its first fandango. He could leap six feet off the ground and stomp and prance like a teenager.

"His kind will never stop," Casey said.

"They broke the mold," Sam said. "Where's Peggy and Adam tonight?"

"Supper with the Wagners and the new preacher."

"Church is fine. I never go into one for fear it'll fall down and kill all those good people," Sam said.

"Churches is for the good," agreed Casey. "Look. Here comes Peggy and Adam now."

Beaver had snatched the dance hall girl from the amused and willing cowboy and was whirling her around, feet off the ground, skirts flying. The cowboy began to clap and now the other customers were picking it up, laughing, enjoying the spectacle. Peggy and Adam Burr and the tall, red-haired preacher, Clayton Lomax, stood in the doorway.

Renee finished the number with a flourish. Beaver hoisted the girl on high, holding her by her narrow waist, then set her down and bestowed a smacking kiss on her cheek.

"Waugh!" He was not a whit out of breath. He reached into his pocket and took out a coin and flipped it to the girl. "My night to howl!"

He wheeled around, conscious of newcomers behind him. He opened his mouth, then closed it again. The pink cheeks paled. He was staring straight at Peggy McLaine Burr. He fell back, making vague gestures with his big hands.

It was Renee who went from the piano to stand with them. She said, "We all saw it. Unmistakable. Peggy, dear, this is your grandfather."

The resemblance, allowing for the difference in gender, was unmistakable. The two stared at each other. Beaver took a half step, then stopped. Peggy's face was hard; she moved close to Adam, seizing his arm in a tight grasp.

She cried, "I don't want no drunk old coot for a grandpa. I don't want anything to do with anybody who'd leave my grandma and my pa and go away and not come back."

Beaver said, "You're her, all right. Jest like your grandma. Never would listen to but one side of anything."

Renee said, "Please. Can't we go to my room and talk about this?"

"I don't care who knows," Peggy insisted. "That's what my folks told me and nobody's goin' to make liars of my ma and pa."

Adam Burr tried. "Now, dear . . ."

She pulled away from him. "Not you, neither. Nobody. He can't come and hang on me the rest of his life."

"Why, baby, I'm bringin' you gold," Beaver said, helplessly, taking out a pouch that jingled with heavy yellow coin. "I don't want to go away. You gotta believe me. Your grandma was mad at me. Said I was a no-good trapper, never had nothin', never would have nothin'. And I ain't never told nobody that till now, so help me."

"That's not the way I heard it." Peggy was adamant.

Beaver appealed to Renee, "What can I do? I been lookin' for her since I fin'lly made a strike. Lookin' all over hill and dale."

"The hell with you!" Peggy was gone out the doors.

Beaver started to follow but Adam interposed. "Sir, I am her husband. We should talk."

The old man's shoulder slumped. He allowed Adam to lead him to the table where Sam sat. Renee joined them. The tall preacher hesitated, then followed, remaining in the background. They settled down in a saloon more quiet even than before. Everyone was trying to stifle his curiosity and mind his own business.

Shaky brought glasses and a beer for Clayton Lomax and retreated to polish the bar within hearing distance.

Adam said, "Mr. McLaine, there is no doubting that you and Peggy are look-alikes. The stories do not match but it is entirely possible that you are correct. I know your wife moved from Taos to work on a ranch. She died. Your son married and was slain by Indians, along with Peggy's mother. Why didn't you return to your family that first year?"

Beaver opened his gaudy shirt. There was a deep scar across his chest. "Got into it with some Blackfoot. Good fighters. They done left me for dead in a gulch near the river. Some Creeks found me. They knowed me. Took a time to git on my feet. Had to trap to get enough to take back. Figured Marg'ret would be over her mad. She allus had that sudden temper. Never could find her, though. Went broke again and went back to the mountains. That's the truth."

Adam, whose termagant mother had done him an unwitting favor by sending him west, was thoughtful. Renee cocked an eye at Sam, who drew a breath, and spoke.

"If I had to swear to it, I'd take the man's word. He ain't got it in him to lie."

A small sigh went around the room. Like children, all wanted a happy ending.

Adam mused, "Peggy needs someone, family. She has moods. If her bitterness . . ." he trailed off.

Renee said softly, "I'll talk with her, Adam."

There was a general silence. Then everyone seemed to speak at once to relieve it. Shaky clattered behind the bar serving drinks. The dance girls set up their customary chatter.

No one heard the horseman in the street. No one saw the object that rolled, sizzling, into the room in the direction of the chair in which Renee sat.

No one, that is, but the old mountain man. He yelled "Waugh!" scrambled from his chair, seized the bundle of dynamite, and ran for the door. The short fuse burned fearfully close to the cap that would blow up El Sol and half the people in it.

He took two dangerous steps. Then he looked before he flung the dynamite into the street, making sure no one would be endangered. The blast singed him. He reeled back, blinking from under the blackened eyebrows.

He smiled serenely at them and said, "Moughty close, that one."

Sam, who had run with Adam to the door, said, "Too close. Did he go south?"

"Yep," Beaver said. "Looks like we ain't got too many friendlies in Dunstan or thereabouts."

Shaky was bringing butter to apply to Beaver's face. Adam was solemn. The preacher seemed undisturbed, a fact Sam noted. Renee was pale, rings under her eyes. The volume of noise now in the town's finest saloon was at an all time high. People came pouring from their homes, recoiling at the damage done to the street. Marshal Donovan was hastily organizing a posse—far too late. Spot Freygang, the newspaper reporter and photographer, was asking questions in rapid fire order. The dog was sniffing at the blast damaged street, for once confused.

Sam said, "You can't win 'em all, Dog. Beaver's got a nose as good as yours any day."

They retreated while Mayor Wagner began to get men together to work on the hole in the street, sending for labor, arranging for light.

Peggy McLaine came in like a small cyclone. She rushed to Adam and threw her arms around him, tears streaming. "I was scared you all had been killed. I was scared to pieces."

"Would have been if it wasn't for your grandpa," Sam told her.

She slowly turned to Beaver. She said quietly, "By the time I got halfway home I knew it was true. I was turnin' back when it happened."

"It is true. No mistaking it," Renee said. "Why don't you go up to my room and talk? Just the two of you."

They went, not touching each other,

tentative, the small girl and the rough man from the mountains. The others watched them until they were out of sight, a warm feeling of satisfaction within them.

Returning to the present, Sam said, "Casey, this is a rangdoodle you got to know about. I didn't think so, but now I know."

Robinson said, "All right, folks. Time to close."

Unwillingly the customers departed. Shaky turned out all but one of the lamps then locked the inner, solid door. They sat at the large rear table, Adam, Robinson, the preacher, and Sam. The dog curled up nearby as though listening.

Sam said, "Casey, somebody's out to kill Renee."

"What? You loco?"

"They tried at the house, my house. Cactus Joe was after her, not loot."

"It don't make sense."

"I thought to keep it quiet so as not to rouse the town. Right now, only the

Burrs and Beaver and us right here are onto it."

"We got to put up a watch," Robinson said. "Renee, we can't do without you around here."

She said, "I hate it. I hate putting you all in such a spot."

"Someone is hiring killers," Sam said. "That's as plain as the nose on my face. The rider that threw that dynamite rode south."

"Dunstan. A bad town."

"Beaver McLaine nosed around down there. He don't know much, but he heard they were after me. I did give 'em some reason, but whether that's important or not I don't know."

"We got to tell the mayor and the council," Robinson said.

"Yes. And Donkey most of all."

"It's too much," Renee said, tears in her eyes.

The owner of El Sol said quietly, "If it was me I'd be glad to have the town on my side. Don't you fret."

They were silent, drinking. The red-haired preacher finally spoke. "Maybe you'd play something, Miss Renee?"

She went to the piano. For a moment she sat with head bowed. It would be her sad music, Sam thought. Then her head went back and her hands struck the keys and the song burst forth.

It was "The Battle Hymn Of The Republic". After the first bars sounded they began to sing the Civil War battle song. For that time there were no Rebels or Yankees among them, only people bonded together.

When it was ended, the preacher said devoutly, "Amen."

Beaver and his newly-found granddaughter came down, arm in arm. They all drank a nightcap together, and the Burrs and the preacher went home. Beaver remained, glowing.

"She said to put the gold in the bank, she didn't need it. She said she was happy. She said she forgave me and all."

"She's a fine girl," Renee said.

"She sure is. Waugh!"

Sam asked, "You looked for her in Dunstan?"

"Yep. Nobody knew nothin'. Found out that Cap Fisher is the big muckamuck 'ceptin' Cy Dunstan owns him, or seems to. Don't figure Dunstan would wanta kill a lady. Don't know about Fisher." He chuckled. "He's fishy."

"You think he's got enough money to hire gunners?"

"No way to tell."

Sam said, "I got to get some sleep."

"Lock up for me," Casey said. He left with Beaver for the hotel he owned. Sam locked the door behind them, turned out the light, and went upstars with Renee. It was a time for comforting and reassuring.

6

IN the morning Renee and Sam stood at the window looking down on Main Street. She was wan, her voice a trifle uncertain.

"Sam, I just can't do it. The whole town. It's just too much."

"Where would you go? They found you here. They'd find you again."

"I don't know. It's unfair."

The dog was in the room, radiating hunger. Sam fed him a bit of a cake. It vanished and the hound looked at him with reproach. Sam said, "Later. I promise you. She'll feed you."

"He's a comfort," she admitted. "All the people and this dog. I know it should make me feel good."

"Think on it. Runnin' wouldn't cut it. Besides I'd have to go along."

"I know you're right." She touched him. "I still hate the idea of involving the

147

town. If only I had a glimmer of an idea who might want me dead."

"Dunstan. It comes from there. I'll find out."

"If there's so much money to hire killers they could get you. Ambush you, as they tried to do me at the house."

"People have been after me for donkey's years," he assured her. "It's nothin' new. The Lord takes care of drunks and fools."

"You're neither." She hugged him and kissed him.

"Looky here." He drew her to the window. The boy called Dink was rolling a hoop down the walk, oblivious of the men at work on the rapidly drying mud hole. Marshal Donovan stood talking to his wife, who held their infant son in her arms. From the general store there emerged Missy Wagner and Clayton Lomax, bearing packages, animatedly in conversation. Wagons were backing up because of the blockage, and the drivers were dismounting to help the workers. The town buzzed with life.

He said, "Those're our folks, Renee. They wouldn't appreciate you takin' off. It'd be kinda insultin', wouldn't it?"

"I am thinking of them."

A wet nose thrust between them. Sam reached down to pet Dog's shaggy head. Spot Freygant set up his camera and began taking pictures of the men working. Peggy Burr came toward El Sol, evidently to talk to her best friend, Renee. Old Abe Solomon from the bank waved at her, and Adam Burr joined him. The sun shot down on all.

"There is no other place," Renee said, half to herself.

"You can run but you can't hide from yourself," Sam told her. "It's up to us. You, me, and Dog. And there's damn few in this burg wouldn't pitch in."

"I know."

"Towns. I been in towns all my life. You see Abe Solomon down yonder? This town was no better'n Dunstan when he come from New York, him and his wife. He had a bit o' money and he loaned it at a low rate and people were able to buy land that he also bought and sold. He opened his bank and Wagner came and Tustin's ranch growed and more money came in. And Abe brought them together, these people. Rafferty's saloon wasn't clean, but then Casey opened this place. And I came in and there was a trouble which you know all about and Adam inherited from the thieves who cheated his dead father. It all happens fast in this country."

"And they welcome strangers on the run," she said. "Like me."

"You give 'em somethin' they need, music. They work hard. The music sorta softens them, makes it fun."

"You're right, darling."

"If that hound could talk." He shook his head. "It's comin' from Dunstan, I know it. Not from the old man. He's tough and crooked enough, but it's not him. That Fisher fella, I smell somethin' there. Old man Dunstan's fooled by him, all right."

"I never knew anyone of Fisher's description," Renee said.

"So he's a hired hand. And there's plenty of money behind him so that he can hire others. Like Cactus Joe." Her face contracted and he said softly, "You got to get used to it, y'know. It's maybe the hardest thing there is. Still and all, you got to swallow it."

"In time," she acknowledged. "It will pass; all things pass." She managed a smile. "Except love, the songs say."

"Believe the songs." He hugged her to him. The dog nestled close, as though demanding its share of affection.

There was a knock on the door. Renee said, "That's Peggy."

Sam held her back. "Is she alone?"

The hound stood at point. Sam drew his gun and asked, "Who is it?"

"Peggy. Who else?"

"Okay." He flung the door open. Peggy Burr jumped in alarm.

Sam said, "Supposin' somebody had her at gun point?"

"I cannot live like this," protested Renee.

"You're goin' to," he told her. "I'm plumb sorry. But that's the way it is."

"Like to scare me to pieces," Peggy said. She was bright eyed, smiling. "Hey, did you see the preacher totin' parcels for Miss Wagner? We asked him to come stay with us. He said the Wagners were so kind. Couldn't refuse their hospitality."

"Now, now," Renee said, smiling nevertheless. There had been a time when Missy Wagner was pursuing, modestly, Adam Burr. "Mama Wagner is head of the committee to build a church."

"Sure," Peggy said, grinning wider. "Sure, she is. And the preacher's a handsome single fella. Sam, Abe and Adam want to talk to you."

"Right. Now you remember, Renee. Keep that gun handy and watch the door. And stay away from the window."

"Yes, dear." She sighed in resignation. "But I can't hide every minute of the day."

"I'm workin' on that." He looked at the hound. "You stay. She needs you more'n I do."

152

He went down to the street and walked toward the bank. The hole made by the dynamite was filled. Sam motioned to Donovan to follow him.

Mrs. Lolly Wagner was a high-busted woman who dressed in black bombazine, wore her hair pulled straight back and walked strictly erect as if balancing a plate on her head. Her view of life was a bit lofty, yet she smiled often and genuinely believed in God and most people. She said to her daughter and Clayton Lomax, "Just put the bundles in the kitchen; the girl will take care of them. Come set down with me and we will discuss the church."

Miss Wagner, willowy, tall, wearing a long plaid skirt and a crinoline blouse, led the way. The parlour was furnished with comfortable chairs, a small sofa, Navajo rugs, chromos of animals and European cathedrals dominating the walls.

"I've always dreamed of a stone church with a tall steeple. I could see Missy walking down the aisle to organ music." She smiled in resignation. "There's stone in the mountains all around us but no means to bring it down. We'll have to make do with timber."

"There is plenty of that," Lomax said.

"And men to cut it. But we need plans. We need a master carpenter. Ours is wounded, shot in the arm." Now her tone was disapproving. "Shot while working on a house for Sam Jones and the woman from El Sol."

"Now, mother," said her daughter. "Renee is a fine lady."

"Who carries on with Sam Jones, you should forgive me for mentioning it, Preacher."

"It's nobody's business but their own," Missy said.

"About building a church," Lomax said smoothly. "I can be of help there."

"Oh?"

"I worked my way through school as a carpenter. It was always that way for me, to work with my hands. Also, my minor at Princeton was architecture."

The two women sat in silent astonishment. Then Mother Wagner raised her eyes and said, "Thank you, Lord."

"You can draw the plans? And help with the building?" Missy shook her head. "It's past believing."

"I may add, I need the work," Lomax told them. "The Lord may be looking down on us all."

"Papa is the treasurer of the church fund," Missy said.

"You draw wages as of this minute," said her mother. "Praise be!"

"Amen." He had reservations better kept to himself. He was new, a greenhorn, and he had notions of his own. He wanted no spires. He wanted a recreation hall where the young people could gather. He believed in music and dancing. He believed that the edifice meant little except as a gathering together of good people. It was possible he had lost part of what churchly folk called "the faith". He could sense the iron in Mama Wagner.

However, he took a quick look at Missy and felt some hope. She was a good girl, not the one he had built in his mind's eye, but one that presented strong possibilities.

Praise the Lord, he thought, but thank Adam Burr, whose letters had enticed him to make the journey westward.

Sam sat in the office of the bank that held his stake—less now than the thirty thousand he had gained from the sale of the Long John mine, presently owned by Adam Burr through a long chain of remarkable circumstances. Abe Solomon, bearded, balding, and benign was sober faced.

"It is a bad time, no?" The banker and town father frowned. "It is for certain of us to consider gravely."

Adam said, "We could get her out of town. Put her on a northbound stage, take her off at night, bring her back here, hide her."

"First place, it might not work. The ones who want her killed seem to know too much," Sam said.

"They could follow. Or have someone

watching all the time." Abe shook his head. "Also, it is running away, no?"

"My sentiments, exactly. She stays and we cover her," Sam said. "Certain people, like Abe says."

"I guess you're right. Dangerous as hell, but it's no good trying tricks," Adam said. "I'm scared."

"Who ain't?"

"Of course they're after you, too."

Sam allowed himself a thin grin. "Never been the time somebody or other wasn't."

"It could be someone from Rafferty's. It could be someone working the mine," Abe said. "It could be, heaven forbid, somebody working for us in the bank."

"Money talks and there's money behind it," Sam agreed.

"If only Renee had a glimmer," Abe said.

"She don't. Never thought to see her like this," Sam said. "It ain't becomin'. Adam, you check those horses in your corral?"

"They are so covered with brands

they're like works of art. They've been stolen so often they wouldn't know their home pastures."

"I'll look 'em over." Sam took from his vest pocket the empty shell Dog had rooted out upon their first meeting. "I got this and the horses. That's all exceptin' some matters my nose tells me mean somethin'. Every smell comes from Dunstan."

"It's not healthy for you to go back down there."

"Not in daylight," Sam said. "Howsomever, there's a few decent people there. And those black men, they're another matter."

"Playing the blues," Adam said. "I've heard about the Negro music. Riverboats carried them north."

"You should hear 'em play. Kinda spooky when they wail. The woman keeps 'em under her thumb. Sooner or later . . . but never mind the music. It's the guns I worry about. The Fisher fella, now, I need to know more about him."

"You think Cy Dunstan is in the clear?" asked Abe.

"I think he's a crooked Abe Solomon," Sam said. "He owns the town, and you don't try to own Sunrise. It's his town in his mind. His son is a joker but the old fella's for real."

"Well, now I think we should tell the marshal what we know, and the council," Abe said. "You agree?"

"I'm afraid the town would get loco if they all knew. One step outa line by anyone would start a riot. Can't have that," Sam said.

"It worries me," Adam said.

"It's a good town but there's always a rotten apple or two," Abe said. "We do know those we can trust."

"You men attend to it," Sam said, rising. "I'll go down to Rafferty's, then to your place, Adam."

"Be careful," the old banker said. The two were like sons to him. He waved as Sam departed and was silent under Adam's pressure to go into action, to call in Donkey Donovan and some others. "All in good time, my boy."

Sam walked down past the repaired section of the street, past the Wagner Hay and Feed company to the district every town would rather be without. Rafferty's Saloon had been in existence before El Sol, when a couple of planks stretched on barrels made a bar for the thirsty, and rotgut whiskey was accepted by all. Rafferty was a burly man scarred by a hundred battles, mean-eyed and belligerent. He stared hard at Sam.

"What t'hell you want, gunslinger?"

Sam said, "I want to ask you about last night."

"Me? What'n hell would I know about it?"

"Anybody you know stealin' dynamite lately? Any stranger in town askin' questions about dynamite?"

"You think I'm loco? You think I want the damn town blowed up?"

"I doubt you'd raise a finger to save El Sol from bein' blown to smithereens."

"You got that right. Far as strangers is

concerned, ain't every rider has the dinero to live it up fancy in El Sol. Ain't every rider wants to. Stuck up, that's Casey Robinson. And t'hell with all of youse."

One of the denizens of the bar snickered. Sam reached over and grabbed Rafferty's shirt and pulled him forward. At the same time he insinuated the muzzle of his revolver under the big man's nose.

"I was askin'. Now I'm tellin' you. Cactus Joe was for sure in here the other day, right?"

"Ugh." Rafferty managed to nod his head.

"Okay. Next time an ugly like him rides into town I want to hear about it. You understand? For your own good."

"Ugh."

"You heard me." He released Rafferty and surveyed the idlers. "That goes for you all. The marshal or me; we want to know."

No one spoke. The place was quiet as the tomb. Sam turned his back on them

161

and walked out. He dared do this for a reason: If Rafferty or one of the others shot him from behind, the shooter would be dead within the hour. They knew this.

There had been times when he had challenged a room full of guns but had backed out the door and moved swiftly enough to save his skin. Walking down the street toward Adam Burr's house he thought about this and how one could sense the odds. Many braver than he had died by not knowing the way men acted under stress.

He relished the sunshine as he went his way, and the greetings of fellow townsmen. He gave Dink a small coin as the kid's hoop ran afoul. Unlike cowmen, Sam was a walker, in his way an interested observer of his fellow men. He heard his name called and saw Beaver coming across the street. They fell into step. The mountain man was again dressed in his worn buckskins.

"Fancy clo'es don't do good with me. Got 'em plenty scorched." His eyebrows were depleted, his face still pink.

"Good thing you didn't have your face hair," Sam said. "You'd have been a human torch."

"Luck. Plain luck. Like meetin' Peggy. Powwowed a heap with her, might say. Made me feel lower'n a snake's belly I didn't ketch up with her sooner."

"Like you say, luck."

"Made me give her the stake to put in the bank. Banks! You reckon it's safe?"

"Safer than totin' it."

"Country's goin' to hell in a hack. Towns, banks."

"Dynamite in a saloon. Somebody after my lady. It ain't exactly tame, now, is it?"

"Been scoutin' around, askin'. Nobody knows nothin'."

"Thought we might look at the horses," Sam said.

"Keerect." They walked a few steps, then Beaver said, "She's cute as a button, ain't she?"

"And good as gold," Sam told him.

"That seems a fine, upstandin' boy she married."

"He's been blooded."

"She told me. A fighter with his fists, is he?"

"All kinds. He'll do to cross the river with."

"Waugh."

The gramma grass grew all around the town on the high plain. Like the property Sam had bought, Adam Burr's acreage was on the outskirts of Sunrise. It was not big enough to graze a large herd, but Adam kept a few cows and was importing Hereford bulls to improve the beef. Longhorn meat was edible and nourishing but required good teeth and patient chewing. They came to the lead-off road and walked gingerly through the drying mud to the corral behind the house.

Blackie Schorr, who was Adam's all around man, came to greet them, a lean figure with scarred features which belied his good nature, a sometime prizefighter who kept Adam fit by sparring with him each morning. He said, "Hey, there. Fine bunch o' goats you brought. I put the

164

mule in the barn; he was messin' up the stock somethin' awful."

Sam said, "Blackie, this is the owner. Beaver McLaine."

"Heard all about you, Beaver. This mornin'. Miz Burr sure is happy to see you."

"Let's take a look at the animules," Beaver said, peering at the four horses they'd brought back. "There's outlaws and outlaws," the mountain man opined. "These here are hoss outlaws. Been stole so many time they wouldn't know their home stable if they walked into it."

Blackie let down the bars and they went into the corral. The horses were restless but calmed down at soothing words. Adam had a high bred harness horse and a couple of cayuses and riding animals. The outlaw mounts were indeed a sorry lot, sturdy enough but showing the effects of ill treatment. Sam went over the botched brands with care. Beaver was not as well grounded in such folderol, he said, satisfied with watching.

"This one, the gray, was once the

property of our councilman, Tillus," Sam said. "Lord knows where the rest of 'em come from. Maybe Tillus knows when he lost one. Doubtful, though."

"I can tell you that," Blackie said. "That TNT brand of his is too easy to alter. He lost three of his'n about a month ago. Riders passin' through. Got such a head start he didn't bother. Mad as a hatter, though."

"So that means Big Mouth and his sidekicks have been hereabouts for some time," Sam said.

"Most likely."

"Reckon I can find 'em," Sam said. He took his saddle down from the corral bar. "Beaver, do me a favor. Tell Renee I've gone lookin'. She'll know."

"Sure will. Needn't say where you're headed."

"You know."

"Get there after sunset."

"Best time."

Blackie said, "Reckon I ain't heard nothin'."

"Adam will find you in. There'll come

166

a time, maybe, when we'll need you," Sam said.

"I'll be lookin' after my animule," Beaver said. "Hasta la vegas."

"Vaya con Dios," Sam said. He worried about the news getting about the town, drifting to the wrong people. There had to be wrong people, or a wrong person, somewhere in the environs of Sunrise. He saddled his hired horse.

The creek that ran down to feed Cyrus Dunstan's ranch had overflown its edges during the storm, creating a marsh that suited the needs of Captain Steve Fisher. He was muddied and triumphant. He had a dozen of the troop ready to drop. They had been out since dawn without food. There were the Dunstan boy, Sven Olsen, several youngsters sixteen or seventeen, and two older men who were under his spell, believing they were readying for a holocaust of some sort.

He said, "Attention!"

They lined up according to height, as he had taught them. Only Kid Dunstan showed true reluctance. He said, "Hey, Cap, ain't this enough? Damn, this is killin' me."

"It's teaching you to stay alive," Fisher said.

"I've learned enough about muck."

They had come to the most turbulent section of the creek. It ran through tall trees, rushing down to the town. It would later subside under the sun which was soaking it up in myriad rainbows.

"You'll learn to cross the river," Fisher said. "This is your chance."

"I don't need it," mumbled Kid Dunstan. "I wanna go home."

"Whining won't get you there."

For a moment it seemed the youth would depart. Fisher stared hard at him. "Your father will hear about this."

No one else spoke. He had control of them; he exulted. They were his, body and soul. He could mold them into a company that would follow him through hell and high water. For this moment he believed he was in a war and commanding a brave and willing combat troop. He demanded, "Who is the best swimmer?"

Kid Dunstan said, "My stomach thinks my throat is cut."

Fisher uncoiled a braided lariat he had been carrying wound around his body. "I want a volunteer to carry this across the stream."

"That ain't no stream; it's a damn river," said the Kid.

Fisher swept them with his hardest gaze. "Who can carry one end of this across the stream?"

No one spoke. He knew he could not force this issue. It was a delicate moment. He said, "Well, then if you're all cowards."

He tied one end of the rope securely to the trunk of a tree. He slowly divested himself of his outer garments, making a neat package of them and handing it to Sven Olsen. Truthfully, he had never been at home in the water. He had learned to swim at the Academy, of course, where it was required. He had not been in moving water since then, by choice. He did not know the depth of the stream he was about to enter. He did not reckon on its force.

He tied the end of the rope about his waist. "When I get to the other side I will tow you over, one by one," he told them. "Any questions?"

Sven Olsen said, "Captain, there's rocks in that crick. They're comin' down hard and fast."

"All the more test of your courage and ability." He knew his shortcomings, had learned them through hard circumstances. He religiously faced them in moments like this. It was part of his overall grand plan. He did not feel ridiculous, standing there in his long johns, stockinged feet in the mud. He was following his star, proving that he could command by example.

He walked upstream, attempting to judge the strength of the roiling water. He took a deep breath and walked into it. He was fifty yards beyond the men who watched in fascination. A stone struck his leg with sudden force and he knew he was in trouble. It was the moment of decision.

If he quit, he would look foolish. If he went ahead, he might be injured, even killed.

He did not hesitate. He plunged into the swift running water. It was icy cold coming down from the high mountains. He had not had time to scan the terrain since arriving in this country. He blamed himself as he gasped and struck out in the breast stroke he had been taught. The rope handicapped him more than he had anticipated. Consigning himself to his dubious fate, he struggled on.

He lost ground from the start. He was swept, fighting, toward the waiting, staring men under his command. He kicked and stroked with might and main to no avail, swallowing water. He tried to keep his head above water and failed.

A round stone detached from the heights above came rushing as if thrown by a giant. He saw it coming. He tried to evade it, diving under in the middle of the current. The rock struck him in the head and he knew no more for a time.

The boys and men pulled on the rope.

One of them said, "The bugger's got plenty of sand."

"In his mouth," Kid Dunstan said, refusing to haul on the lariat. "Let him go, good riddance."

The others persisted, Sven with one hand, unwilling to drop the clothing in the mire. They hauled him to the shore and dragged him through the mud to safety. Water gushed from his mouth. The lifted him, face down, and he choked and gurgled and stared at them, regaining consciousness. There was a red ring about his body where the rope had cut into his flesh, and blood was on his face.

They managed to remove the water-logged underwear and socks. They dried him as best they could. He coughed and choked and regained his speech.

"My clothes," he whispered, conscious that no man could command when naked.

Sven helped him on with his garments minus the underwear. He drew an agonized breath and said, "So I failed. We learn through our mistakes. Nature was stronger than me." He paused. "Does anyone else want to try?"

No one spoke. He had not, he knew, lost their respect. He took a step, staggered and would have fallen had it not been for the hand of Sven Olsen. He shrugged himself erect and said, "We will return to our base."

Another man came to support him. They walked slowly toward town. He was sore all over. Every step was an agony, but he never faltered. Experience had taught him that it was possible to maintain respect through failure. He bit down hard and held onto his dream.

They sat in the library of Philip Barnes Merrivale, a high-ceilinged room in a Fifth Avenue brownstone mansion. The walls were lined with books that had been read. Deep leather chairs accommodated the two men. There was a decanter of fine wine between them. The senator, Barnes Emerson Merrivale, caressed his short, white beard and said, "Philip, I tell you I agree."

"I must impress it upon you, Uncle. The conservation bill must pass. You are really not interested."

"The West is still raw. And—it is not important to my constituency. However, I repeat that the bill will go through. And you will make another fortune." He smiled and poured wine into imported Venetian glass. "Keep cool. 'It will all be one a hundred years hence.'"

"Ralph Waldo Emerson."

The senator from New England sighed. "I miss him. I miss Henry Longfellow."

"They hated each other. They made their mark and died almost together. As Emerson said, 'Every hero is a bore at last.'"

"You've been brooding again. You have everything a man needs including half the women in the city. They throw themselves at you. You are handsome and healthy and rich. And young. If I were your age . . . ah, if I were your age!"

"I remember when you were my age. And Uncle Ralph and Uncle Henry . . . and father," Philip said.

"Yes. And you were a rascal always except later, when you were with her."

"Playing duets." Philip shook his head. "A fool in love. And still in love."

"You lost her. Must you spend your life trying to find her? How do you know she would be the same? Philip, you are wasting your time grieving for that girl. She's a woman now. Can't you find someone else? What about the other one?"

"She wanted marriage. I could not marry her."

"She was a strong woman. Her family was wealthy. She was very handsome," the senator said.

"Too strong," Philip said. "No. Not while my lady is alive."

"The Pinkertons cannot find her. She may be dead."

"No. I would know if she were dead."

The senator shook his head. "A millionaire sentimentalist."

"You see, I have always loved her. Since we were children."

"I know." His uncle spoke kindly. "I

respect your love. Your father was a one-woman man. Still, you should not live alone."

"'Nothing can bring you peace but yourself.' Mr. Emerson again."

"'The world uncertain comes and goes, the lover rooted stays.' We can sit here and quote our betters all night. Have your man call my carriage. I'm leaving for Washington tomorrow. Again, your bill shall pass. I promise you."

Philip saw his uncle to the door. A heavy fog had rolled in so that the street light shone blue on damp paving. It was a night for snug love, he thought, retiring to the music room where the butler brought the wine. He sat down at the grand piano, knowing he was hurting himself, unable to refrain.

He played Beethoven. He remembered her sitting beside him, their hands touching. He could see the long, slender fingers caressing the keys. He could never play as she did, but he had the affinity for music.

The other woman, now, she was a

dancer, graceful, sexual. She had filled a time when he was striking out, hurt, damaged. Then she had made the mistake of trying to take over, to discharge his faithful servants, to run his life. He had discovered a hard inner core to her. He had told her that he would never marry while his first love was alive. It had, finally, been enough to drive her away.

He was good at that, he thought bitterly, driving them away. He had been headstrong, selfish, wanting it all without giving enough. He had increased his inheritance by using that characteristic in business. He had learned when it was too late that the only gain was through giving. He should have listened to Uncle Ralph Waldo Emerson. He should have listened to Uncle Barnes, who had taken his father's place after the War. He could not remember his mother, who had died when he was an infant, but he had been loved and cared for by some of the greatest men in the country, who had coddled him and tried to influence him.

The failure had been his own. He faced

it, pounding the keys of the piano in a fierce crescendo of his own improvisation.

Renee was at the piano. Casey Robinson sat where he could watch the door, a Colt .45 in a holster worn high on his hip. Marshal Donovan made his stop and spoke to him.

"I got Sandy Stone sworn in. He'll be patrollin' outside."

Casey said, "Adam'll be in later."

"The mayor and the council will be in for the poker game. They know about it."

"Shaky's got his shotgun oiled behind the bar. You take care of outside; we'll be ready in here."

The dog lay beside Renee. It was dark over Sunrise. The regulars were all on hand except for the councilors, who were having a meeting regarding the new church. Renee played on, going from popular tunes to the classics, not knowing which, her mind culling her past with diligence, unable to find a clue that would in any way produce anyone who would want to kill her. Certainly not her first love, that flamboyant boy and man of many parts. She had left him long ago. She went through the dark passages and bright ones in her memory. No one, she thought desperately, was a killer.

Someone—it may have been he, the first one—had put the Pinkertons on her but they had proven easy to avoid. A change of name, swift moves on the railroads had taken care of them. They were mainly slow-witted bunglers, she had learned.

The council filed in and Mayor Wagner came to her. She stopped playing as the kindly man said, "Miss Renee, we are goin' to take care of you. Believe me."

"I believe you."

"What with that peculiar hound and Sam and all, we got you covered."

"You are the best people in the world." She spoke with heartfelt emphasis. "I am ashamed that I should put you to such trouble."

"Ain't no trouble betwixt friends. You have lifted our hearts with your music.

179

We're plumb proud of you," the mayor said.

Tears moistened her eyes. "If anyone is hurt . . ."

"When you're on the watch it ain't easy for anybody to try what's been tried. You sure you ain't got a notion?"

"Dead sure. I'd give anything if I did."

"What can't be helped must be endured." He patted her shoulder and went to the poker table. He was trying hard not to show the concern that they all felt, she knew.

Out of the corner of her eyes she saw Long John and Ike Simson, two of Tustin's cowboys, come through the door. She played their favorite dance tune, "Buffalo Gals". They waved to her but went to the bar. Tustin had brought them in to help protect her, she thought. It did not make her feel any better. Those hardworking men needed their fun. She finished the number and went to her table in the rear, Dog on her heels. She sat down and Casey came over, bringing a bottle of whiskey. They poured, and she felt the drink all the way down to her toes. It did not help.

Adam Burr came in. He was wearing his gun, which was unusual. She was altering the habits of everyone, she thought. The preacher and George Spade followed Adam and all gathered at her table. Casey poured for them.

Adam said, "Clay is a carpenter. He and George will work together on the church. Clay can also draw the plans. Some preacher we have here."

"That's real good news," Casey said.

Renee's mind came back to the present. "Could you take a look at Sam's house also?"

"Why . . . I'm looking for work of any kind." Lomax straightened his back. "You people."

Adam said, "George can use two good hands. He's walking around complaining that time's going by and nothing's done."

"You bet," the carpenter said. "Golly, if there's a death you could he'p me with the buryin', too."

Lomax swallowed, then said gamely, "I could do that."

So it was decided. Renee tried with all her might to put her mind to the building of the house. It was a good try, but it did not work.

What it did do, she realized, was bind the new preacher to Sunrise and its inhabitants. She could see it in him, the realization that he had come to a place where he was accepted at face value. Friends, she thought; here were the greatest of friends, a blessing she could cling to in the absence of Sam Jones.

They had taken Steve Fisher to the Dunstan place. The women had attended to him. Vera Brazile was with him in one of the upstairs bedrooms.

"I can't appear to be weak," he said. "I must be up and about."

"You can't be up and about. You brought it on yourself. Now you must rest."

"I will make it. They must see that I am strong enough to overcome disaster."

"There's no disaster. Merely an accident." She smiled at him. "You will remain here until I release you."

He reached out a hand. "I would be a willing prisoner."

She drew back. "No. I told you, no, until the business here is finished."

"It was not so on the riverboat."

"Where you were gambling away your money."

"Where you hired me."

"You've been paid."

"I gave you what you wanted."

"What do you mean, sir?"

"I worked for you. I found your prey," Fisher said.

"You also failed me."

"I am not finished with that."

"You had better not be. That is why I am here," Vera Brazile told him.

"Everyone else failed you."

"Granted. That is not the point. We have an agreement. There can be nothing between us until it is settled."

He said, "It will be accomplished."

"I am not wealthy enough to hold out

much longer. Associating with these churls is not my idea of life, you know."

"Nor mine. Yet there is opportunity here. Great opportunity. We could do as well in Dunstan. Establish a position of power." His eyes glowed. "There is no limit in this country."

"At this moment there are stumbling blocks. There is, for instance, the man Jones."

"Nothing. An ignorant gunman."

"My dear," she said, "you have ambition, that is good. But you have limited vision. The man Jones is not to be dismissed. He is far more than he appears."

"I saw you charming him on the dance floor. I did not realize he was charming you."

"Jealousy is not becoming to you. The man is a force. Take care."

"I will be ready when the time comes."

"Make sure your bully boys are on hand."

He said, "I'll not need them."

"Pride goeth before a fall. Rest now,

take care of your health. I need you, Steve." She leaned to kiss him on the cheek.

He said, "You are a strong woman, Vera. We can go far together. You must have been terribly harmed in the past. It will all be forgotten when we succeed."

"Yes. When we triumph."

She left the room. He was only partly a fool, she thought. He was certainly brave. If he had what it took all would be well. He was lacking in many respects. He could be fooled if he was offered power. She did not want power. She wanted a man and the man was not Fisher.

She had been orphaned early. There was money enough to pursue her career in the ballet, but she had lost interest when she sprained an ankle. A life in New York society had become her utmost desire. Then she had met the man. The affair had been swift, and she had loved him. At least she had loved him as far as her nature allowed. She wanted him; she wanted what he could give her. It was not the same dream as that of Steve Fisher. It was position she craved. It was ironic that here, in this miserable western town she had position. How they envied her, these crude women of the West. How easy it had been.

It would be simple to go with Fisher's dream, even to marry him if necessary. She was aware that she could twist old Cy Dunstan around her finger if it came to that. Tough as he was he could be flattered into doing anything she desired; it was his only weakness. Fisher would be a slave . . . he was right about the opportunity to be found in this country, but he too had the weakness for a woman like herself.

They did not know her. She was obsessed. There was iron in her that could only be heated by getting that one man. It had been tempered by the mixture of love and hate.

Sam Jones called upon his total recall of terrain once traveled. It was a dark night; only one star twinkled in an otherwise clear sky. He rode circuitously to the cabin of the black musicians. He tied up his horse to the thin tree and made his way to the window. They were again playing the music of their own. Pompey was crooning. He stood for a moment, soaking it in. He heard the cry for freedom, for lives of their own. When they stopped to drink from their bottle he called to them.

"It's the man from Sunrise."

There was a profound silence.

"I want to talk some more," he said.

"You got anything for us?" one of them whispered.

"I've got ten dollars."

"I hears you, man from the town sounds like heaven."

A hand reached out. Sam put ten dollars in it. He said, "Heaven it ain't. Better than this hole, though."

"Anything would be!"

"There's no watchman here. How come?"

There was a chuckle. "Boss man, he

bunged up. Lady boss, she got him over to mayor's house."

"How do you know that?"

"Gets around."

They called it "the underground" during the War. The downtrodden and have-nots always knew what was going on in the world. Word of events spread like wild fire.

"What happened?" Sam asked.

"Boss man tried too hard. Got hit inna head. Tryin' t' swim when he shoulda been thinkin'."

"When's the next dance lesson?"

"Soon. Boss lady ain't said."

"You boys okay?"

"Got vittles. Got likker. Got music."

"I'll be sashayin' around. Stay strong."

"Ain't no t'other way, Mister Sunrise."

"I'll be talkin' with you." Sam went back to the horse. The musicians were enduring better than most men would, he thought. He rode the back way to the Olsen house. He went afoot to where there was a light and called.

Sven answered. "That you, Mr. Jones?"

"It ain't my brother. What happened to Fisher?"

Sven said, "He bit off more'n he could chew. He's got sand, though, gotta give him credit."

"Just where's his place?"

"You go straight south. It's adobe, low and kinda deep. Better watch yourself."

"Your brother with you?"

"No, he's with Cassie Dixon."

"Can I borrow a pry bar of some kind? And a candle?"

"Sure." There was a tool shed in the back yard. Sven came with a lighted candle and they found the required tool. Sven said, "You goin' to break in?"

"I'm looking for something important."

"You want help?"

"No. I don't want you boys in this thing. It's enough you're on my side."

"We don't like what's goin' on, Mr. Jones. Somehow it don't seem right."

"Just stay home and keep quiet for now. I appreciate it."

Sam left the black horse under an oak tree and walked. It was difficult in the dark, in strange territory, but his cat eyes stood him in good stead. If he stumbled, he regained balance; his instinct kept him on a direct course. It was a night as black as any he could remember. After what seemed an interminable time he could distinguish the house described by Sven, a vague outline. He came to the north wall and felt his way along to the rear.

There was the sound of men walking. He flattened himself on the ground against the house. Figures came to within a few yards of where he lay. He drew his gun and held his breath. The two men paused, almost invisible, shadows against deeper shadows.

A voice said, "Darker'n a bull's belly with its tail down."

"Sure is. This is a dumb job."

"Cap's mighty tetchy about his house these days, ain't he?"

"He's got the wind up, all right."

"He looked good out there this mornin', though."

"He looked damn bad if'n you ask me."

"He come out of it good."

"You reckon?"

"Sure. Never whimpered when we was totin' him down to Dunstan's."

"After he made a fool of hisself."

"That's what it takes, like he said."

After a moment the second man said, "Mebbe you're right."

"Cap, he's got the right notion. Git ready for anything."

"Takes too much of my time."

They moved, walking slowly to the front of the house. Sam had no desire to attack them; he had nothing with which to tie them up. He waited until he thought they were safely out of hearing and darted to where the rear door must be located.

He used the pry bar with dispatch. The portal gave, cracking. He poised, ears ringing with the sound, still unable to see clearly in the black night.

191

There was no sound outdoors. He slid into the house. He replaced the door as well as he could, making as little noise as possible. He put the pry bar at its base. It was blacker than the night inside the room, which he determined by touch was the kitchen. He groped his way along the walls. The blinds were drawn tight. Even in the darkness he felt the orderliness of the place.

He took a taper from his vest pocket and lit the candle. Again he waited. For the first time since he had quit smoking years before he wished for a cigarette. He took a deep breath to steady himself down.

He moved into the next room. He saw a man staring at him. He drew his gun and almost fired. Then he realized he was looking into a full length mirror.

His laughter, stifled but deep, brought him back to earth. Captain Steve Fisher had a looking glass in which to admire himself. How many knew of this phase of the hard man's character?

Sam shaded the candle with one hand

and looked around the room. There was the sparse furniture, hard floors. And against one wall there was a gun rack. He pounced.

One by one he conned four rifles—two Winchesters, one the 1873 model center fire, the second the latest make; an Enfield, and a Remington. He examined the hammers, holding the candle as close as possible without dripping wax upon them. That wax fell upon the polished floor he cared not. The broken door would reveal that someone had broken in.

The weapons were in mint condition. There was not a scar on any one of the hammers. None had fired the shot that had so narrowly missed Renee.

I could be, he thought, on the wrong track.

On the other hand Fisher undoubtedly had had a rifle with him earlier that day when he took his men on maneuvers.

He prowled through the rooms, noting the sparse furnishings. Fisher was a character of a sort he thought he knew. The man tried to live hard in order to make himself hard. It was a condition to question—whether to admire or suspect.

It was fruitless to look further. Sam went to the door he had unhinged and picked up the steel bar. He edged his way out, then tilted the door so that it closed. He snuffed the candle and was turning when two arms enfolded him from behind.

He writhed, kicking backward. Someone swiped at his head with a gun barrel, nearly knocking him out. He flailed, realizing that he was caught between two of them, that he had not a chance in a thousand of getting free.

He made one last desperate, writhing, fighting attempt. Then he relaxed, hoping they would fall for the old wrestling trick and loosen their hold.

It seemed to work. He was free. He spun and struck with the pry bar.

He felt it go home. He flailed again. The second man emitted a hoarse cry and fell away. Sam struck again and he was free, and the two were down and not stirring. He felt around in the dark, breathless from the struggle. He managed to locate each man's gun. He removed them, emptied them, and threw them away as far as he could.

It had been stupid to back out of the house, he thought. He had been lucky. He retraced his steps. He found Midnight and rode back to the Olsen house. Sven was waiting in the back yard. A wind came up at last. He shivered, sweaty from his exertions.

Sven said, "I was worried."

"You had a right to be. Howsomever, here's your bar and your candle."

Sven said, "Got a telegram. My folks are stranded in Texas by a storm. You want to sleep here?"

"No. Like I said, it might get you boys in Dutch. I'll sneak into the hotel."

"Oley hasn't come home."

"I'll look for him. Thanks for helpin'."

"Wish I could do more," Sven said.

"Maybe you can some time."

Sam took the back way. The wind increased and now there was a sliver of moon to light his way. He put the black horse in the stable behind the hotel and unsaddled and found some grain for the feed box. He went around to the front of the hotel, uncaring now whether or not he was seen. There were, he knew, people in the shadows. There was neither sound nor movement. They remembered the last time, he supposed. He entered the hotel and found Oley and Cassie in the dining room.

Cassie said, "It's Mr. Jones. I knew he'd be back."

"You sure got your nerve," Oley said.

"You mean I'm not welcome?"

"Heck no. I mean after what happened and all. Set down. I'll get you a drink. Mr. Dixon's gone to bed, we're in charge."

"I'd like some vittles if you could find 'em."

"That's my job," Cassie said. "They'll be cold, though."

"My belly won't know the difference," Sam told her.

Oley brought a bottle. "Anything you want to know, Mr. Jones?"

"I'd admire to have you drop the mister. Plain Sam'll do."

"Sven's at home."

"I know. Your folks are stuck in Texas. Cap Fisher got a knock on the head."

Oley said seriously, "Sven told me. You know he wanted to send one of the men in that river. He's like to get somebody hurt bad one of these days."

"I wouldn't doubt it."

The twin went on, "Me and Sven, we been talkin' about it. Cap and that dancin' lady got old Dunstan by the short hairs, looks like. The mayor's a tough old bird but maybe he can be fooled like anyone else."

Cassie came with cold cuts and fresh bread and butter and coffee and cake. They talked. Sam worried that Oley might be seen with him, then decided it would be considered a chance encounter. It was a time for relaxation after a long, hard day.

No western town was without its Rafferty's Saloon. It provided an oasis for the down and out, the disreputable, the saddle bum. It reeked of stale smoke and liquor fumes. Over the bar was a chromo of a reclining, near naked odalisque to stir the dreams, fly specked and slightly awry. Behind the bar, which was scarred and slightly sloped, Rafferty loomed, dirty shirt open, unshaven.

Three Mexicans gesticulated, spouting rapid Spanish, waving their arms. Suddenly one drew a knife. Rafferty walked without haste to the scene. He seized two of the participants by the scruff of their necks and banged them together. He kicked the third in the groin. He then threw them out, one at a time.

A dilapidated cowboy said, "Seems like you couldn't afford to do that, Rafferty."

There were only two customers remaining, the speaker and a waif asleep in a corner.

Rafferty said, "What I do, I can do. T'hell with it."

"Gimme a drink." The man counted out coins. "Last one for me."

Rafferty poured rotgut into a four ounce glass. It was his boast that he never cheated on drinks; he gave the full tot.

He said, "Finish that one and the house'll buy."

The man tossed it down. "You got your good points all right. I'll say that for you."

"You better had. I don't take no guff."

"You oughta have as much business as that fancy joint down the street. Robinson's so stuck-up he won't allow honest people in the place."

"Don't you worry none about me. I got my ways."

"You're a good man, I don't care what they say." The cowboy drank the free offering and staggered out into the night where the moon had just made its appearance.

Rafferty came from behind the bar and kicked at the feet of the last customer. The man started up, staring wildly about.

Rafferty said, "Go sleep some place else."

The man croaked, "Ain't got no place to sleep."

"Here's two bits. There's a Mex flophouse four places down. Don't go uptown or the damn marshal'll have you in a hoosegow."

"Thankee." The man wandered out. Rafferty locked the door. He reached under the bar and poured himself a glass of whiskey no customer would ever taste. He went into the bare back room that contained two chairs and a table with the bottle in one hand and two glasses in the other.

He thought about the cowboy's remark, "I don't care what they say." He had accepted it as a compliment, now he knew it was not. They said things about him, that was for sure. It had never been any different.

He had been a street kid in New York, one of the Five Points gang. There had been a riot and the police had caught him stealing from a broken shop window. A lousy cheap pistol it had been and they had beaten him and thrown him in jail.

When he was released they had chivvied him until he knew he had to leave the city.

He had come west and found his career selling whiskey to the Indians in North Dakota. When he had accumulated enough cash he had moved south out of the cold winters and eventually to Sunrise in its infancy. He had been through battle with Sam Jones and others and had barely survived. He nursed a grudge that racked him to the bone.

There was a tap on the back door. He opened it and the expected visitor entered, a dark man, thin and of medium height, wearing a black hat and a mustache to match. He wore sweat-stained brown pants, brown boots, and a brown shirt, under a Mexican serape which he doffed as he sat down hard in the chair Rafferty had vacated.

Rafferty said, "I was expectin' you, Frank."

"Hell of a ride, back and forth, back and forth."

"If it wasn't for the dinero, we'd both quit, wouldn't we?"

The man called Frank took out a small pouch and tossed it to Rafferty. It clinked solidly with the sound of coin. Rafferty caught it and put it in his pocket and filled the extra glass with whiskey. "The good stuff. What you wanta know?"

"The usual."

"Jones is in Dunstan."

"Damn. I must've missed him."

"Now y'know. The dame? Just try to get near her. The whole goddam town is watchin' over her since you tossed that dynamite into the joint."

"That figures. Anything else?"

"They got a new preacher. They're gonna build a damn church. The town's gone to hell altogether."

"Who cares? All I want is news of the dame. This here's the lousiest job I ever hired on to do and I've had a few."

"I bet you have. Well, you're better off than Cactus Joe."

"Joe wasn't the worst sidekick in the country. Kilt by a damn woman. Ugh!"

"That woman's got the town by the butt. Her and that damn Cemetery Jones carryin' on," Rafferty said.

"You gettin' religion for the new preacher?"

"Huh! Thing is, any other woman behavin' like that, ev'body'd be hollerin' and yellin'."

"Y' can't count on nothin' no more," Frank said.

"Only this." Rafferty jingled the coins. They drank, and Rafferty went on, "You never can say where this comes from. Right?"

"Right. I aim to live."

"Must be plenty of it."

"Seems so." Frank closed up, staring at the ceiling.

Rafferty raised his glass. "Up the Irish, Maguire."

"How'd you know my name's Maguire?"

"You told me when we was drinkin' that time."

"Up the Irish."

Rafferty said, "Must be plenty of dinero in Dunstan."

Frank Maguire shook his head. "Best you shut up and take the money. Mind your own damn business."

"So long as some of it comes my way. Mebbe I'll move to Dunstan when this is finished."

"Make sure you live to make it there," Maguire said. "I got to sleep. These rides are killin' me altogether."

"You know the way."

"You sure you don't know anything that'll help?"

"I'm tellin' you, she's got the town watchin' and a stinkin' dog followin' every step she takes. You'd need an army to get to her these days."

Maguire finished his drink. "I'm goin'. Keep your eyes and ears open, Rafferty."

He went out the door like a wraith. The man was spooky, thought Rafferty. He would lead his horse, spent from the ride, to a certain squalid Mexican shed where it would be fed and cared for. In the early morning he would be gone with the wind.

He was a born killer, Rafferty knew, like his partner Cactus Joe. There were a few of them left in the country, and they could be hired by anyone who could afford them.

He blew out his lamp and went upstairs to his bed. Killing a woman wasn't something he would think of on his own. However, he had no compunction about the riddance of anyone connected with Sam Jones—or El Sol.

Clayton Lomax sat at the kitchen table with a drawing board, a T-square, and a triangle plus a dozen pencils, all provided by the indefatigable Mama Wagner. Across from him was Missy Wagner, eyes bright, watching him begin to design the Sunrise church.

She said, "Mama is really upset about the spire and all. I don't see how you convinced her."

"Your mother is a discerning lady. She realizes that only so much can be done in the beginning."

Missy hesitated, then said, "Mama has

her problems. Papa goes to the poker game at El Sol almost every night. I think she hopes she can get him to meetings in the church when it's built."

"My idea is to make it a gathering place for all."

"I know. That's why Mama went along with your plans. But you don't know Papa."

"Time'll tell." He bent closer over his work. "You can't force religion upon anyone. That's why I left the traditional church, you know."

"Yes. Well . . . Mama wanted me to ask you about that."

"What about it?" He leaned back and looked at her.

"Well, were you ordained?'

"No. I have my degree, Doctor of Divinity. Isn't that enough?"

"For me, oh, dear yes. And for all of Sunrise. Adam Burr said you were his friend. That's good enough."

"Mama had doubts," Lomax said.

"Not really. The preacher who rides the circuit, he probably never saw a college. It's just she was raised Methodist. She sure argued with that fellow when he came to town. You see, with the two of us to keep house, she has a lot of time on her hands."

"I understand. Anything else she wanted to know?"

"Well . . . you drink beer and all. You're a lot like Adam." She blushed. "I mean, you both come from the same place. Lawsy me, was he a pilgrim when he landed here."

"Pilgrim?"

"That's western for a stranger. Mainly from the East. Adam wore the strangest clothing. He was—he seemed to be—greener than you."

"He was a wild one in Princeton. We sparred together. He's strong as a young bull."

"Oh, yes. He fought here once. When we were having trouble."

"I heard about the trouble from him."

"No matter what Mama says about Sam Jones, he saved the town. Adam, too."

She giggled. Her rather plain face lit up

so that she was pretty in the soft light. "You're not like a preacher at all. I bet if you were here during the trouble you'd have been fighting along with the others."

"Thank you, I think." Now they were grinning at each other, attuned. "I believe in religion and fun. I don't see how you can have one without the other."

"Do you play poker, too?"

"Now that's where I draw the line. I wouldn't look so good sitting in El Sol holding cards and smoking a cigarette, would I?"

"I can just see Mama's face!"

"I wouldn't blame her. A true preacher is supposed to marry, stay home with his wife and children—unless he's on church business."

She sobered. "What else is there for a nice *girl* to do in Sunrise? That's why Peggy McLaine—" She stopped, biting her lip.

"Peggy? Adam's wife?"

"I shouldn't talk about her. We're not real friendly but . . . I shouldn't say."

"I'll learn about her sooner or later. Better I should be warned, possibly?"

"She lost her folks. What could she do, marry a cowpoke? Wait on tables if she could get the job?"

"So?"

"She was—a dance hall girl."

"Something in the way you say that makes me think there is more to it," the preacher said.

"Well . . ." Her voice trailed off, she flushed.

"I think I see."

"She's a wonderful girl. Adam loves her dearly. Her best friend is Renee Hart. Renee teaches her—lots of things. She loves Adam a heap."

He reached out to touch her hand. "What you are saying is that you cannot find it in yourself to pass judgement. That is truly fine."

She did not remove her hand. "They say the West is hard on women and dogs," she said dryly. "It's true, you know. Even the dog that Sam Jones found is treated better than Peggy McLaine was."

"It's changing, isn't it? For the better?"

"Yes. Mama doesn't give enough credit to Sam Jones and Papa and lots of other men, but they try."

"We can hope the church will help." He returned to the drawing board. "Now what do you think about the roof? What's best for this country?"

"Wooden shingles," she said. "Peaked roof."

"Just what I had in mind."

She said, "Would you like to hear about the trouble? It's a fierce story. Our old marshal was killed."

"Tell me. You tell a story very well."

She beamed and began to tell the tale of how Sam Jones had sold the Long John Mine to a pair of swindlers who had then enlisted outlaws to rob the bank and take over the town, and how Adam had fought the giant black man and Sam had used an old cannon to foil the invaders, and how Adam had inherited the mine and other moneys because one of the swindlers had murdered his father.

She had a nice light voice, and he listened with great interest until Mama Wagner called her daughter for bed.

The night stage rattled into Sunrise. Marshal Donovan was waiting in the shadows. A drummer climbed down, then a tall man wearing a drooping mustache, city garb, and a long Colt dangling in a filigreed holster. Donkey stepped into the light from the station.

"Howdy, mister."

"Howdy, Marshal." The man's voice was low, steady.

"Name of Donovan."

"I'm Earp. Wyatt Earp."

"The hell you say!"

"Just passin' through. I heard Sam Jones was livin' hereabouts."

"Sam's outta town. But there's folk would like to shake your hand, Mr. Earp."

"Is there a poker game goin' in town?"

"Nothin' that would interest you. Dollar limit. The Mayor and such."

"Let's look at it."

"Too bad Sam ain't here. Let's go over to El Sol. Folks will be glad to meet Wyatt Earp."

The famous man of Abilene and Dodge City grinned. "There's plenty wouldn't admire that meetin' too much. However a thirst is a thirst and a game is a game. Lead on."

On the way across the street Donovan asked, "Any chance you stickin' around for a while?"

"Nope. Have to meet Bat Masterson in Arizona. Town called Tombstone."

"I heard about the place. Got some troubles there."

"No problems of mine. Just meetin' Bat and Luke Short for a go-around."

They came to the swinging doors of El Sol. Renee was playing Mozart with variations of her own. Earp stopped and listened. When she had finished he said, "Heard music like that in New York one time. Only this here's different."

"Renee, she's somethin'," Donovan said. He added, "She and Sam, they're close."

"Thanks for tellin' me." Earp took another long look at Renee. "That's Sam all over. He always did have the best taste in womankind."

The occupants of the saloon were now staring at Donovan and the tall man. Donovan announced, "Folks, this here is Wyatt Earp."

Mayor Wagner came from the poker table. "Welcome, Earp, welcome. Come have a nip."

Donkey Donovan said, "'Scuse me, folks," and tore himself away, back into the streets lighted by dim kerosene lamps, but still lighted, a big step forward in the history of Sunrise. He was in his twenties, probably the youngest marshal in the West. He had been trained by the veteran Dick Land who had been killed in the trouble the previous year. Donkey was married and had a child. He was sturdy and conscientious and had the confidence of the town.

213

His deputy had been working the day shift, therefore the marshal was in for a long night. He walked Main Street, knowing every inch of it, every nook and cranny of the byways. He noted that Rafferty's was closed early, not for the first time. This would have been a good thing except that there had to be such a joint as Rafferty's. Those not welcome in El Sol had to have a place of their own. He knew this and regretted it but had no solution. He did not bother his practical mind with the problem. Several doors past Rafferty's there was a light in the house of Francesco Diego, a man to be suspected of any small crime, a sometime bartender for Rafferty. He thought of knocking on the door and reflected that Francesco was not truly dangerous and continued his round, turned, and started back. He needed a dozen deputies, he thought, and then realized he had that many, counting the people who knew about Renee and were watchful. He wondered for the hundredth time who would want to kill that nice lady. It was far beyond his imagination. He could only do his job.

There was a light in a window of the Wagner house. The new preacher seemed like a fine fellow. A church would be a good thing, Donkey thought, not that he was religious, nor was his sturdy farm girl wife, but all and all, lots of people wanted a place to worship.

He walked down past the blacksmith shop where the historic cannon was covered against the weather. He came back to his office behind which were empty prison cells and unlocked the door and trimmed the wick on his lighted lamp. He came out and went diagonally across the street and past the bank to El Sol. He went in and ordered a beer from Shaky and wandered to the poker table where Wyatt Earp was sitting in with the members of the town council.

A hand of stud was in progress. There was perhaps ten dollars in the pot and only two players were left, Mayor Wagner and Earp.

Earp showed a king and no pair.

Wagner showed a queen and no pair. Earp's hat was tilted over his nose; his concentration was complete. Wagner's face was expressionless. One would imagine there were hundreds of dollars at stake.

Tullis was dealing. Earp drew a trey, matching nothing, leaving him king high. Wagner drew a trey, matching nothing, leaving him king high. Earp drew a deuce with the same result.

The mayor said, "Your bet."

Earp studied his hand, then that of his opponent. He drawled, "Lemme see. Everybody bet, then dropped. You stayed without a raise. This here is complicated. Have you got a pair? Have I?"

Wagner said, "Your bet, Wyatt."

Earp said, "Okay. I bet a dollar."

"Raise a dollar," Wagner said, stony, cold.

"You paired," Earp said resignedly. "Well . . . I call."

Wagner turned over his hole card. It was a queen, giving him the pair.

Earp sighed. "I should've knowed. Still, a man's got to find out for sure."

Wagner was triumphant. He crowed, "Now I can tell my grandchillun that I won a pot from the great gambler Wyatt Earp." He raked in the money. "Drinks are on me."

Earp said, "Plenty people won pots from me, Mayor. Can't give you another chance, I'm afraid. I have to get some sleep before takin' that stage tomorrow morning."

They all drank and they all wished him well. He went to Renee and bent over her hand in the most courtly fashion and said, "I wouldn't have missed your music for a dozen pots. Give my regards to Sam, all of you, please. A very good night."

Donovan accompanied him to the hotel. He asked, "You got any advice for a green marshal?"

Earp fingered his luxurious mustache. "Tell me, Marshal, would you have played that last hand like I did?"

"Well . . . no. But y'see, I'm onto the

mayor. He never stays in unless he has 'em."

"Nevertheless. You got to know when to fold 'em. Luke Short, he'd have dropped out. Bat Masterson too. And Sam Jones is a faster draw than me. And you broke in under Dick Land, one of the best ever lived, rest his soul."

"Well, but . . ."

"But me no buts, Marshal. You can shoot straight, they tell me. Sometimes that's better'n a fast draw. Make sure. Most quick ones shoot without aimin'. That's about the only advice I can give you."

"Dick Land, he told me that."

"He had a hand in my younger days. Give my very best to Sam now. Make sure," Earp said.

"You might could catch him in Dunstan."

"Wish I could. But Bat's waitin' on me. Good night."

"Good night and a pleasant trip."

Donkey watched the tall man enter the hotel. One of the best-known figures in the land and his advice had been stale. In fact, he had admitted being wrong. Maybe that was a lesson in itself. Suddenly he no longer felt too young and too new at his job. He settled himself in to watch the doors of El Sol lest another attack be made upon Renee. It was not as lonely as it had been before Wyatt Earp had come to town.

EARLY in the morning Kid Dunstan was donning his spurless boots. The plump girl amidst the tangled bedding in the house of ill repute said, "Y'know that gunner from Sunrise is in town, doncha?"

He stopped dead with the second boot in his hand. "How the hell do you know?"

"He came in last night, seems like. He was seen goin' into the hotel. He was with Oley Olsen."

"You seen him and didn't tell me." He swiped backhand at her. "You all know I wanta know when he's seen."

She had ducked; her aplomb was undisturbed through practise. "You didn't ask."

"Do I got to ask about every damn thing? I told you and everybody." He yanked on the boot.

She whined, "You didn't pay me, remember?"

"I ain't goin' to, now. You don't do as I say, you don't get no money."

"Kate'll see about that."

He snorted. "Kate hell. My old man owns this building." He would have to get another fancy pair of boots, he thought. A heel on his good ones was broken by the bullet Sam Jones had fired. He almost struck the girl again, then cursed her and went down rickety stairs to the parlor. There were three slatternly girls and Kate, the madame, in the room.

He said, "Why didn't one of you tell me Jones is in town?"

Kate stared stonily at him, the wreckage of a one-time beauty. "Because you were drunk as a skunk when you got here."

"I wasn't all that drunk." He had been, at that. He had escaped the family and Vera Brazile and hit the bars with Doodles and Monty, two of his drinking buddies.

There was a clatter on the stairway just

then and his companions came stomping down. Doodles had on his fixed grin; Monty was beetle-browed, carrying two guns. Both were bleary-eyed. They gave money to Kate and Monty said, "Drink, I got to have a drink."

Kid Dunstan said, "I'm agreeable."

They went out and their horses stood with heads down, panting. They had neglected to loosen the girths or remove the bridles.

Doodles said, "That's the first time I ever done that."

Kid said, "Hell, my old man will murder me. Let's take 'em to the livery stable."

They walked the dazed horses across the street and left them to be cared for. They went into the nearest bar and ordered the best whiskey. It was none too good but their thirst was greater than their taste buds.

Kid Dunstan asked, "Anybody in here see that bastid from Sunrise last night?"

"He was seen," the barkeeper said.

"Whereabouts?"

"In the hotel."

"Alone?"

"With one of them Olsen twins and the gal."

"Cassie Dixon?"

"Nobody else."

"Give us another shot."

They drank. The Kid said, "We could go to the hotel."

Monty said, "You do that."

Doodles guffawed. "Cap sent four men after him. You know what happened to 'em."

"Yeah. Apaches? You believe that story?"

"You're scared of him," the Kid said.

"Yeah. You ain't?" Doodles retorted.

He forbore a reply. Those two knew him.

Monty said, "The Olsens, now that's a different horse."

"What about them?"

"Seems like they're kind of friendly with Jones. You didn't see it at the dance lesson?"

"Nope. Hey, bartender, you got

somethin' to eat in this joint?" the Kid called out.

"Could rustle up some eggs."

"Okay. Let's have another hair of the dog here."

They drank up. "Them twins, they ain't one of us," said Kid Dunstan.

"One of 'em's got the redhead gal you was after," Monty said.

"She ain't nothin'." But it rankled the Kid. He tossed down the whiskey and poured another. "Mebbe we could get somethin' about Jones out of the twins."

"Worth tryin'."

The eggs came and they wolfed them down and had another drink. Now they were swaggering even as they stood at the bar.

"One of 'em's always home while t'other's cuttin' meat," Monty said. "Can't tell 'em apart nohow."

"That don't matter. What one knows t'other knows. Damnedest thing I ever see," Kid Dunstan said.

"Their folks ain't home," Doodles put in.

"Let's ask some questions," the Kid said.

They had another drink and left the saloon. They walked past the hotel and peered into the butcher shop to make sure one of the twins was working. They went down the alley to the rear of the Olsen house and hallooed.

It was Oley who answered. He looked at them and asked, "What's up?"

"We're up. Wanta know somethin'," Kid Dunstan said.

"Like what?"

"What's that Cemetery Jones up to, is what?"

"How would I know?"

"You was with him last night."

"He didn't tell me anything."

"You Sven? Or Oley?"

"Oley. What of it?"

Kid Dunstan said, slurring his speech, "You and Cassie Dixon, you think he's somethin', that Jones."

"Well, ain't he somethin'? You ought to know."

It was the wrong thing to say. It struck

225

at Kid Dunstan's overweening vanity. He let out a wounded yell and threw a wild punch.

Oley ducked. Monty grabbed his left arm and twisted it behind him. Dunstan struck again, hitting Oley at the nape of his neck. He sagged.

Now, the liquor heating them, they all pummeled the helpless twin. He tried to fight loose. Monty hung on, kicking at his legs.

Kid Dunstan delivered one more crushing blow upon the now unconscious form. There was a cracking sound.

Monty released his hold. "Hey, I think you broke somethin' there."

Doodles said vacuously, "I heard somethin'."

Oley lay on his back, sightless eyes staring at the sky. They leaned over him.

Doodles said, "Geez, he ain't breathin'."

Monty felt for the pulse of the stricken youth. "It's beatin'. A little."

"We better get the hell outa here,"

Doodles said. "His old man'll sure have us kilt."

"His old man ain't around," Kid Dunstan said. He jumped back and fingered his gun. "Maybe we oughta kill him so he can't talk."

"You loco or somethin'?" asked Monty. "There's people get nosey when they hear a gun. Let's get the hell outa town, Doodles."

"Hell of an idea."

"What about me?" The Kid was almost sober, watching the two of them go back out of the alley. "Hey!"

"It was you started it." They were gone.

He yelled after them. He stood on one foot, then the other. He was not good at making sudden decisions. He knelt beside the still body of Oley. He touched the white face. It was cold. Panic seized him.

He dashed to the mouth of the alley. There were a few people about. He ran back past Oley and stumbled across the back lots. He fell once. He got up and managed to make his way to the livery stable.

His horse was standing in the corral but the mounts belonging to Monty and Doodles were gone.

He fumbled with his saddle, muttering words that made little sense to the attendant boy. He mounted and rode wildly toward the ranch and his mother.

Sam Jones ate a leisurely breakfast and talked with Cassie Dixon and her father. He learned about the mortgage held by Cyrus Dunstan.

"He about owns the whole town," Dixon said. "No way to get from under his thumb."

Cassie added, "Where'd we go, anyhow? You say you got a fine hotel in your town."

"That we have," Sam said. "Old Cy's got everyone scared around here. Long as you can meet the payments maybe it's better you hang in."

"Thing is, Dunstan's always talking it up about the town growin' and all,"

Dixon said. "If he got throwed off a horse and broke his neck we'd really be in it. Think if his wife and that damn Kid was runnin' the shebang."

Cassie said, "Please don't even mention it."

Sam said, "Perish forbid. I better be gettin' along."

"I'll walk a ways with you," Cassie said.

"To the butcher shop," said her father.

She made a face at him and he laughed as she walked to the street with Sam, a tall girl in a long calico dress, youthful as springtime, the sun shining on her freckled comely face.

Sam said, "I'd better get on with it quick."

"Are you plannin' on seeing Mayor Dunstan?"

"Probably. What I'm lookin' for is a rifle with a nicked hammer," he told her. "I know that don't make sense to you."

She was looking down the street. "There's Sven, comin' from the shop."

She called out and the twin came running to them.

"Something's wrong with Oley," he said, scowling.

"What is it?" She was instantly alarmed.

"I don't know. I always feel it, we both do, when something's wrong."

"Is he doin' the chores?"

"Yes, it's his turn." Sven started toward the Olsen house, Cassie and Sam on his heels. People stared at them as Sven began to trot. They came to the alley and the twin dashed ahead to where his brother lay on the ground. Cassie uttered a cry of horror and rage as she ran to kneel beside the unconscious Oley.

Sam said, "Don't touch him. Looks like bones are broken."

She snatched back her hands. "He's been beat up."

"Looks like it." Sam was gently feeling the chest and shoulder of the boy. "One of you better get the doctor."

Sven said, "I'll go. I can run faster."

Tears were streaming down his cheeks. "He's alive, ain't he? I know he's alive."

"He's alive. Looks like he was hit hard back of his neck. See the lump?"

Sven said, "So long as he's alive," and was gone, sprinting.

Cassie's voice was muffled but steady. "Whoever did this is goin' to die."

"Now, now. We'll know when he wakes up."

"How do you know he's goin' to wake up?"

"I've had some experience with broken bones," Sam said. "Better a doctor, though."

She said, "I love him so," and began to cry, sobbing without sound.

Sam examined the earth around Oley. The markings were plain as day. There had been three men. The scuffle had been brief. One had certainly held the twin while the others beat on him. The despicable attack had taken place not very long ago, probably within the hour. He did not want to leave the girl while he went to ask questions . . . which would be of dubious value in this town anyway, he thought. Time enough when Oley recovered consciousness, as he had told the others.

The girl had stopped weeping, still kneeling beside the unconscious boy. Sam looked at the battered features as she gently wiped blood from them and the gnawing, deep passion that he experienced before action began to burn his innards. His voice was deep in his chest when he told Cassie, "They'll pay the fiddler, don't you wonder. Time's a-wasting for these people in this town."

"There's too many of 'em," she said dully.

"There's an old sayin'. 'Be quiet, be sure, be loyal and move.' Movin', that's my part. Think of the rest of it, Cassie. Hang on."

She bit her lip. Color was returning to her face. "So long as he lives."

He was impatient to move, but he leaned against the wall and considered which way to go. There was the threat to Renee. There was this terrible wrong against a decent and friendly young man. There was the force of the town against himself, one man.

The sun was directly overhead when Sven came with a young medico, bearing a stretcher made of two poles and rolled canvas. "Dr. Fox," Sven said. "Please, tell us how bad it is, Doctor."

The young man produced a stethoscope and examined Sven's chest. "Strong heart," he muttered. He felt of the body with expert hands. "We had better move him into the house. It would be dangerous to carry him farther."

Sam helped. The girl followed them as they struggled through the door and into a bedroom that contained two cots, one for each of the twins. The neatness of the house was impressive. Sam remained while the doctor completed his findings.

"Broken arm. Probably broken collar bone. A slight concussion. He may remain unconscious for a time. I can set the arm and bandage him. He'll need nursing."

Cassie said, "He'll get nursing."

"He will need medication." The doctor took out a pad and pencil and began to write. Sam edged to the door. The doctor was dressed in a frayed blue jacket and trousers a bit too tight. It was not a time to ask questions as to his loyalty. Better to go into action.

Sam departed without goodbyes. He walked back to the main street and stopped by the butcher shop, to inform the man named Pate what had occurred. Then he went to the hotel, where Dixon was behind the desk.

Sam said, "Bad news. Oley was beat up. You'll want to see what you can do. Your sweet daughter will have to nurse the boy."

Dixon said, "Damn! That stinkin' Dunstan kid I bet. He's always been jealous of the twins, 'specially Oley."

"I'll be tryin' to do something about it." Sam left to walk across the street and stop in the telegraph office. Asking for help was something he had never done and he had to search his mind for the right words. Finally he said, "Mister, I can read your key. You savvy?"

The middle-aged operator said, "You want to send a message? Send it."

Sam recited it slowly. "Beaver McLaine. Sunrise City Hotel . . . You mind where we picked up the horses . . . Meet there tonight . . . signed 'Sam.' Want to read that back?"

"You're Sam Jones," the operator said. "Don't you worry none. It'll go like you say."

"Send it." Sam put a five dollar bill on the counter.

The man said, "You don't need to over-pay."

"Glad to hear it. There's some scared folks in this burg."

"I ain't one of 'em."

"Glad to hear that." Nevertheless he listened while the message was tapped out. The time had come when he could believe no one in Dunstan except the twins and the Dixons.

Satisfied, he went to the stable and saddled up Midnight. He mounted and rode for the Dunstan ranch, the road to which was plainly marked. Beaver was the only man in Sunrise he could call upon with a clear conscience, he thought. Adam was newly married and settled down. He could scarcely ask Donkey Donovan to desert his job. There were no other real fighting men in town. Brave men, but family bound and proper for use as defense only.

Two men against an army—it was plain foolish. He had faced odds in his life but this was the biggest gamble of all. The old Mountain man was the best he could imagine . . . if he lived to meet him at the deserted cabin in the woods. Beaver had no responsibilities; he loved action; he was tougher and smarter than anyone Sam knew.

He came to the wide open gate of the ranch, over which was an ornate filigree of iron which sported the brand, D Bar D. He rode the circular driveway and tied up his horse to the hitching rack. He went up on the porch and before he could knock a maid opened the door.

He entered to find Cyrus Dunstan grinning at him.

"Saw you comin', Sam. Glad you could visit."

"Not a real visit," Sam said. "Got bad news."

"Come in and have a drink and tell me all about it. We're just about to eat. Glad to have you join us."

Mrs. Dunstan and Vera Brazile were in the parlor. Sam remained in the hallway. "Three men beat up Oley Olsen. Real bad."

"Beat him? One of the twins? Whatever for?"

"Not the point, is it, what for? You tell me Captain Fisher is the law around town. I heard he was here, came to let him know about it."

Fisher came down the stairway. He was wearing a light bandage around his head but appeared to be steady on his feet. "What's this? Someone hurt?"

"One of your young men," Sam said.

"Oley Olsen," added Dunstan.

"We'll see about that," Fisher said. "Any idea who did it?"

"Just a notion," said Sam. The anger was boiling and he fought for control. He spoke directly to Dunstan. "Did your son come home within the hour?"

"Why . . . I dunno." But the mayor was on the alert.

Fisher said, "I've been resting. Had a bit of trouble." He touched the bandage lightly.

"I heard," Sam said. He took the cartridge with the nick in the rim from his pocket. "Like to have you two take a look at this."

Dunstan turned it in the light. "Got a mark. Hammer mark." He handed it to Fisher. "See it?"

"Uh . . . why, yes."

Sam knew in that instant that it was Fisher's gun that had fired the shot at Renee. He controlled himself—he could not be certain that it was Fisher who'd had the gun in his hands at the time.

He said, "Whoever owns the gun

knows who took a shot at the lady in Sunrise."

Dunstan said, "Now that's a circumstance. How you goin' to find that partic'lar gun?"

"That's my problem," Sam said.

"Mighty big one, seems to me."

"Problems keep comin' up," Sam said. "I wanted to keep you informed."

"I just don't see how we're consarned," Dunstan said, frowning.

"About the Olsen boy? Or the gun?"

"Well, now the Olsen boy, that's definitely ours," Fisher said. "The gun—I don't see how we can help."

"Truly, I didn't expect you would. But the gunner rode this way, y'see. Thought —but then youall said you didn't know anything about it."

"That's right. Meantime, you sure you won't have a bite with us?" Dunstan was insistent in his hospitality.

"No thanks. I'll be runnin' along."

Fisher said, "I'll be in town later if you're still here."

"I'll be around."

239

Before he could escape Vera Brazile came gliding into the hall. "Is that you, Mr. Jones? If I'd known you were coming I'd have scheduled another dance."

"Nice of you ma'am." He was anxious to get away from all this fooforaw.

"Maybe we can arrange it?"

"I doubt it. There's things to attend to."

Fisher said, "The man's in a hurry. I think we should let him go."

"Thanks." Sam backed out of the door. He heard voices as he went down the steps. He stopped dead.

Someone was yelling, "That damn kid ruins every hoss he rides. I'm sicka this muckin' around."

Sam walked around to the back of the house. A stocky man was saying, "You do like you're told, Babbit. Or you hit the trail."

Sam said, "Speakin' of horses, ain't you missin' some?"

The man named Babbit wheeled around. His hand started down toward his gun butt, stopped halfway as he stared into the muzzle of Sam's .44.

"I dunno what you're talkin' about, stranger."

The burly man said, "Now, take it easy. You're Cemetery Jones."

Sam said, "I don't like the name."

"Whatever. We don't want shootin' on this ranch."

"This ranch hires some crummy hands, seems like."

"My name's Vaughn. I didn't hire him nor his pardners."

"Then the owner oughta be more careful."

"Cap Fisher took on these bums," Vaughn said. "You got anything you can say to get rid of 'em?"

Sam said, "Could be. Don't see any sense in it right now. Is that beat-up nag the one young Dunstan rode in an hour or so ago?"

"Why, yes, it is. What of it?"

"A young man got hell beat out of him by three brave ones this morning. One of the Olsen twins."

241

"Shoot, they're nice boys, the Olsens. That's too damn bad," Vaughn said.

"Where's young Dunstan now?"

"Sleepin' it off, I'd say. No use to try him whilst his ma's around."

"I agree. Well, sometime later."

Vaughn said, "Reckon you know it ain't healthy for you in town."

"Nor out here, seems like."

"Nobody's goin' to pull any underhand stuff whilst I'm around," Vaughn said. "Cy Dunstan's my boss and he don't hold with much neither."

"You know, I believe you." Sam had seen Babbit backing off. Now he was making for the barn.

Vaughn asked, "What was that about Babbit's horses?"

"You might tell him we've got four nags with worked over brands in Sunrise."

"I don't get your drift."

"It ain't the time. Let me give you a piece of advice. When the war starts— stay here and be out of it."

"War? You're kinda het up, ain't you?"

242

"You could say that."

"Well, let me give *you* a piece of advice. Don't try to start any war around this shebang," the foreman said.

"If young Dunstan beat on Oley Olsen I might not have to start it." Sam estimated this four square man and made a quick decision. "How do you stand on Cap Fisher?"

Vaughn scarcely hesitated. "I'm agin him."

"Okay. I've already put a bug in your boss's ear. If what I think is true, Fisher will be out of here some day soon. What about Babbit and his three pardners?"

"Trash." Vaughn added, "They could be dangerous."

"Any tramps with a gun is dangerous," acknowledged Sam. "One more matter. Fisher's house was broken into last night. You hear anything about that?"

"A rider come out with his head bandaged. Matched Fisher's head."

"Then it augurs that Fisher knows but ain't makin' it public."

Vaughn said, "I'm always behind you

but I'm beginnin' to catch up. I'll have words with Cy. Been with him a long time. I can't stay for true which way he'll jump. He does listen to me about cattle. That's my business, cows."

"Reckon we understand each other, Vaughn."

The man put out his hand. "I know your reputation, Jones. And I don't mean as a gunfighter. Do what you must."

Sam rode toward town convinced that he had talked with an honest man, pleased that he had imparted enough information to accomplish his intent: to keep Cy Dunstan quiet and out of his hair. On the other hand there was the problem of young Dunstan. Nothing was assured. The rage within him had settled to simmering rather than boiling. He debated his next step as he rode.

Young Dunstan snored, emitting alcohol fumes. Fisher shook him awake with difficulty. He yipped and threw out his arms.

244

Fisher demanded, "Who was with you when you beat Oley Olsen?"

"Monty and Doodles," stammered the youth, not yet fully wake. Then he coughed and said, "What you talkin' about? I don't know nothin' . . ."

"You dumb ass. Don't you lie to me. Where did the others go?"

"Uh . . . they run off." He was scared now, shaken, rubbing his eyes. "My head aches. Mama has somethin' she gives me when my head aches."

"Never mind your mama. Cemetery Jones is on your trail. When and if the Olsen boy wakes up you might as well figure you're in jail. If he dies, you're dead."

"What does Jones know?"

"He knows plenty." Fisher's mind was traveling at top speed. "Too damn much. I swear, I don't know what to do with you. One thing, don't you dare leave here. Not until this is settled. If you do, you'll wind up dead as sure as the sun rises."

"Nobody's gonna kill me. My old man . . ."

"Nobody can save you if Jones is after you. Put that in your thick skull."

"My head's bustin'."

"I'll send your mother. You mind what I say, now. Do not leave this ranch. In fact every time you go outdoors it could happen to you." He made a slicing motion with his hand across his throat.

He went downstairs knowing that he had not made an impression on the dull sensibilities of young Dunstan. It was impossible to get through to the fool. He spoke to Mrs. Dunstan who scurried up to her only offspring. Vera Brazile stared at him in quick alarm.

"You look as if the world was coming to an end," she said.

"Where's the old man?"

"He just went out to ask Vaughn what Jones was talking about. Jones and Vaughn had a long conversation while you were upstairs."

"The time has come for action." He

strove to control his agitation. "We have to do something at once."

"I am all for that. Have you decided what should be done?"

"Jones has to be killed."

"We knew that," Vera Brazile said.

"You were right. He's smart as a snake. He got the old man to thinking. Lord knows what he said to Vaughn. I'm certain they talked about Babbit and his bunch. Babbit's a liar and a thief."

"You hired him."

"What I did is past. What I do now is what counts. It comes down to that, lady."

"Careful, my friend. It sounds as if you are taking the bit in your teeth, so to speak."

"That's as good as anything to believe." His voice was low and hard. "It's no longer a question of your money. It's life or death."

"You have all those men under your spell. How is it that you can't take care of Jones?"

"That is precisely what I aim to accomplish."

"So?" Her voice was equally harsh. "And what about that which I aim to accomplish?"

"Jones must go first. Surely you can see that."

"You do believe you can kill him?"

"There's no other way."

"For each of us." She nodded. "He's in town. Therefore you can get to him."

"You heard about the rifle. I've got to get to him soon."

"You're the law."

"He broke into my house last night. I now know that. He's looking for my rifle with that defective hammer I didn't know about. I'll not be carrying it. You must hide it or destroy it for me."

"Yes. I must." She shrugged. "Although how I do that I have no idea."

There was a touch of desperation in him now. "If he closes in on me it will lead to you."

"You think he's that clever?"

"You agree."

248

"I do. Very well. First things first. Go and do the job," she said.

"Is that all the encouragement you can offer?"

"This is no time for sentiment. You have your goal, I have mine. You either go forward or I find someone else to do what I want done."

He eyed her and felt himself turn cold. She was not the least bit interested in him, she was all for herself, every last smidgen. He said, "Yes. I see."

He went to his room and dressed and buckled his gun belt. His superb physical condition asserted itself; he felt no ill effects from yesterday's accident. He went down to find Cy Dunstan and said, "I'll resume action, now."

"You got well quick." Dunstan was perturbed about his son. Sam Jones had indeed had an effect upon him.

"I will check on what happened in town."

"You do that. I want to know."

Fisher went out to the yard and

approached Vaughn. "What did Jones have to say?"

Vaughn said shortly, "Nothin' you'd wanta know."

"I do want to know."

"Sorry. Got nothin' to tell you."

"Your boss'll hear about this."

"That don't shake me up none."

"I'll want a good horse."

"There's the corral. Help yourself."

The man was defying him but he had no recourse. He roped a dun mare and saddled her, a horse he knew had bottom. He mounted and rode out the ornate gate toward town.

Sam stood by the bed in which Oley lay. Sven sat with hands clenching and unclenching. Cassie walked in stony-faced, unshed tears in her eyes, bearing a cold cloth, which she placed on the brow of the unconscious twin.

"He's breathing regular," Sam said. "Good sign."

"If I knew where the others went . . ." Sven said.

"They'll turn up."

"I'll kill them."

A bubble appeared on Oley's bruised lips. His eyes fluttered, then closed again.

Sam said soothingly, "He's comin' around."

"Or dyin'," Sven said, his jaw muscles working.

"No! Don't you dare say that," cried the girl.

A blanket of silence fell as they all leaned toward Oley. He opened one eye. "Wha . . . that you, brother?"

Sven said, "Thank the good Lord in heaven!"

Cassie came close and leaned to kiss the black and blue face. "Talk to us, darlin', talk to us!"

"Hey, there." The voice seemed to come from a far place.

"Who did it?" Sven demanded.

The faint smile turned to a frown. "The Kid."

"And who else?"

"Doodles . . . Monty . . ." The eyes

closed again. "Gotta rest. We'll get 'em . . . Cassie?"

"I'm here. I'm right here."

"I'll be . . . be . . . all . . . right." Oley drifted off. A bit of color had returned to him.

"Now you know," Sam said. "He's goin' to live. Describe the two besides Dunstan to me."

Sven tried. Cassie interrupted, "Doodles looks like he was born dumb. Monty looks like a black devil."

"I'll know 'em." He started for the door. "Take good care of him and yourselves. Keep the door locked and a gun or two handy. They may want to get at him again."

"So he can't tell on 'em," Sven said. "I'll be ready." He took down a double barreled shotgun from the wall. "I'll load it with buck. I'll blast 'em in two if they come here."

Cassie said, "Get me a gun."

"Keep a watch," Sam told them. "I'll be back." But he knew that a surprise attack in force could overcome them. He went to the black horse and mounted. There was too much time before Beaver could arrive. He had to do something profitable with that time.

He rode to the neighborhood where the musicians dwelt. There were people around. He dared not be seen near the cabin. He sought a place to leave the horse where it might be safe. It was the time to take chances.

He had once read in one of Haldeman's Little Blue Books, that had come free with Bull Durham tobacco before he had quit smoking, a story called "The Purloined Letter" by a writer named Poe. The sought-for missive was in plain sight in a drawer, overlooked by the searchers. He knew Fisher's discipline had slacked off when he had been hurt. He put the two thoughts together and rode a wide perimeter around the cabin. He saw no outposts. He dismounted beneath the skinny tree of his night visits. He walked without haste to the window and called, "It's the man from Sunrise. Open your door a crack."

He sauntered as though to pass the door, then ducked inside. The voice he remembered as being Pompey's said, "Man, you crazy. Have a nip."

The interior was as neat as a pin. They had managed to whitewash the walls, and there was a faded rug on the dirt floor. In the only other room, spacious enough, there were three beds made up and clean. There was a stove in the kitchen-front room, and chairs wound with wire and a bench on which sat the other two, the fiddler Hambone and the horn man Jeb. They grinned at Sam as he accepted the bottle and took a sip of very bad whiskey.

Sam asked, "What have you heard lately?"

"Town's a buzzin' 'bout the Olsen boy. Town knows you was there to he'p. Two bad boys rode no'th." Pompey was the spokesman as always.

"You think the kids with the blue shirts won't stick with Fisher now?"

"Cats don' run with dogs."

"There's enough dirty dogs without the cats," Sam said. "Still and all it would be

254

good if none of the good boys got hurt."

"You goin' to start up." It was a statement, not a question.

"Any minute. You be ready."

"Fo' what, like?"

"For anything."

"Lady sent word maybe a dance tomorrow night. Maybe even tonight if she can get to the people," Pompey said.

"Any way you could spread the word to the people?"

"Nigger he'p. Messican he'p. All stick together."

"Put out the word," Sam said.

Pompy was puzzled. "Why you want dancin'?"

"Keep folks off the streets. Maybe bring the goddam Dunstan kid to town. Lots of reasons."

Pompey shook his head. "You somethin', you man from Sunrise. You gonna put the bad ones in the cemetery I bet."

Jeb picked up his horn. Hambone put the fiddle under his chin. They began to play a tune Sam had not heard before.

"What's the name of that one?" he asked.

255

"Funeral tune in N'yorleens. 'When The Saints Come Marchin' In.' It's gen'rally played after the buryin'."

"It ain't that sad." They had picked up the pace.

"It's for when yo' is *comin' home* from the funer'l." Pompey spread his hands. "Le's hope on it."

Sam unbuttoned his shirt and pulled out a waterproof money belt. He took bills from it and handed them to Pompey. The other two stopped playing, their eyes as round as saucers. He said, "Just in case, there's enough to get you out of town."

Pompey asked, "Wha' for?"

"The music," Sam told him. "The music helps. Never stop playin' it."

He opened the door, looked, saw no danger. He waved to the still-stunned musicians and went to his horse. He was on a roll, he thought, just acting as if nothing could deter him. He rode back to the main stem and tied up at the general store. He went in and there were people doing business but they seemed to pay no heed to him. He found a bandoleer hanging from a rafter. He bought enough ammunition to fill it. He carried it out to his saddlebag. He led his horse to the hotel. Dixon was behind the desk.

Sam said, "I must be invisible. Nobody's takin' shots at me today in broad daylight."

"The town may be owned by Dunstan but mortgages can't buy hearts," Dixon said soberly. "What happened to Oley has got into 'em."

"Do they know who did it?"

"They got a notion," the hotel man said. "They seen the Dunstan boy ride south and Monty and Doodles ride north. They know all three was drunk as skunks the night before. People put two and two together. Then they stop and think suppose it was them."

"I believe their notion is correct," Sam said. "What are they goin' to do about it?"

"Set on their hands. Fear is stronger than wantin'."

Sam said, "I want to pay my bill. I'll

take my bedroll. It don't mean I'm not comin' back."

Dixon said, "If it wasn't the old man's son."

"Right."

"I sure hope you can do somethin'. I don't see how."

"Alone I haven't a snowball's chance in hell." Sam paid his bill. "If you'll put me up some grub?"

He took his bedroll and a bag of food outside to the saddle. He mounted and rode north. The sun was lowering; he had plenty of time to reach the cabin on the hillside. He thought hard about ways and means. If he could locate the pair who had been with Kid Dunstan he might gain some ground. He might bring them in and force Fisher's hand. They were Fisher's men, he had to be responsible. If he could separate Fisher from Dunstan . . . it came down to Fisher, he knew. He had failed to find the rifle. He could not be positive that Fisher had fired upon Renee. He still couldn't imagine any reason why the man should have done so.

Therefore, he thought suddenly, Fisher may have been hired.

Unless . . . unless under another name Fisher was part of Renee's past and unbeknownst to her had reason to want her dead.

Fisher was Dunstan's man and surely the mayor had no vendetta against Renee.

He was going around and around, he realized. There was a cog missing in the machinery of his skull. Until it was fitted into the puzzle he had to work on instinct and pray for luck.

He came to the turnoff as the sun was drooping down into the western hills. He loosened the girth of the horse and removed the bridle so that it could graze. He ate sparingly of the cold food provided by Dixon. He hunkered down with his back against the ramshackle cabin and prepared for another time of waiting.

Vera Brazile said brightly, "Isn't it wonderful how quickly we can gather our friends?"

Mrs. Dunstan said dubiously, "Not as

many as last time. Dixon and his daughter won't be there nor the Olsen twins. I dunno, there is somethin' funny goin' on, seems to me."

"Nonsense," said the dancing woman. "There'll be enough people to learn the pattern of the cotillion."

Cy Dunstan, slightly tipsy after a huge meal and several whiskeys, said, "Might's well have a good time."

"Captain Fisher ain't goin', neither," complained his wife. "I swear I don't know what all's goin' on."

"Better get ready to leave," the mayor said. "Time's a-wastin'."

"I don't see why my boy can't go." Mrs. Dunstan sniffled. "Why does he have to stay home?"

"Far as I'm concerned he can go. We got so few anyway," Dunstan said. "Make an exception." He paused, then said darkly, "Not that he mightn't be in trouble again."

"He says he doesn't want to attend," Vera Brazile said.

"He ain't stayin' out here all alone."

260

Now Mama Dunstan was decisive. "You tell him, Cy. He's gotta go."

Amiable, draining the last of his drink, the mayor said, "Whatever you want, Ma."

Vera Brazile smiled. "Thank you. We do need everyone we can get. The music will make us all feel better. Music and the dance does away with all woes."

She wanted them in town; she wanted them where she could watch and possibly sway them. Fisher was gone to the wars. It could be, at the least, the end of Jones. If that were accomplished the rest would be possible, even probable. Jones was the lodestone, the stumbling block. If she had realized that in the beginning—but that was Fisher's fault. He had not finished his spying. He had found the woman but had neglected to learn enough about her.

It was a new starting point. Fisher was hard enough and mean enough, she thought. She composed herself for the evening. She could hear the bellicose tirade from upstairs.

"I don't give a continental damn what

261

Fisher says. This here dancin' is what we got in Sunrise, you understand? This is what gives us high society doin's. Every time we do this I send out word to the big cities. Waltzin' in the town of Dunstan. We got to grow and you got to grow with the town, whether you wanta or not, you better believe it."

The response was weak. The fool boy would be with them. Not that it made much difference, she thought. Nothing in the big room behind the City Hall would make any difference to her that night. All she wanted was to have Sam Jones dead and out of her way. Then the coup—and her return to eastern society.

Frank Maguire said, "He ain't in town." He was worn to a frazzle, his cheeks sunken, his eyes dull. "I rode myself to death gettin' here. Had nearly no sleep. No news from Rafferty that's any good."

Fisher's head throbbed with pain. "He must be on his way back. We'll go after him."

"Hell, he'll be long gone ahead."

"He stops halfway at that cabin where Babbit got stung." Despite his pain Fisher felt the adrenaline flowing. "The bastard broke in here last night. Laid out Jason and Amby. You hear about the Olsen twin in town?"

"Same time I heard Jones had left. The fool Dunstan kid. The other two are campin' in the hills. They'll be ready."

"Good. We've got Babbit and his three. Jason and Amby. Four others I can count on. I'm keeping the Dunstan brat out of it."

"No loss. Can I ride your gray?" Maguire asked.

"Certainly. Take care of your horse, leave him in my stable." Things were working fine in his head. "This will be a posse after Jones."

"What's the charge?" Maguire grinned.

"Beating the Olsen twin."

"Can you make that stick?"

"Jones can't deny it if he's dead."

"If the twin lives he can tell on Kid Dunstan and the others to a judge."

"The mayor's son?" It was a weak

spot. Fisher said, "If it comes down to it the Olsen boy will have to go."

"Want me to take care of it before we ride out?"

Fisher turned the offer over in his feverish mind. He shook his head. "Too dangerous. There'll be people nursing him. Can't take the chance."

"Whatever you say." Maguire was indifferent. "I'll saddle up. Best get ridin' if we're to catch him."

Fisher said half aloud, "And when we do, you and I will ride on to Sunrise."

"Finish the job." Maguire nodded as he left.

Fisher watched him, the perfect instrument he had found right here in Dunstan through chance. Maguire had been broke and hunted when Fisher was new in town, organizing his troops. Desperate for a stake Maguire had joined up. In a jiffy Fisher had recognized the lack of morality, the coldness that ran to his soul. They were a lot alike, he knew. The difference lay in Fisher's yearning to reach a goal. Maguire needed only women and a few dollars and someone to rob or kill or maim. If there ever was a completely evil, cold killer, it was him. He would have to be eliminated when the job was done.

Perhaps Jones would do it for him before then, Fisher thought.

And what of the dancing woman? Could he master her after the job was finished? He doubted it. He would not need her if he could keep control of Cy Dunstan by convincing him that there was need for the troop and his, Fisher's, services. Leaving Kid Dunstan and the other boys out of tonight's expedition would help.

He did not want to give up on the woman. On the other hand, she was too positive, too single-minded, too stubborn. Too . . . strong.

He made himself concentrate on the matter at hand. Sam Jones must die.

The night was growing cold. Sam shifted his position for the hundredth time, shaking his head to keep awake. He heard the sound of a four-legged animal coming up the path and rose to his feet, loosening his revolver in the holster.

"Waugh."

There was the patter of paws and Dog came hurtling to him. He said, "Beaver, what the hell? Dog was supposed to be watchin' over Renee."

Beaver rode Mossy the mule to the cabin and dismounted. "Your lady's bein' watched over by near the whole town. She sent the hound to you for luck."

"He's been luck, all right. Set and let me fill you in."

When Sam had finished Beaver said, "Hard to tell just which way to go, ain't it?"

"Want to augur that with you. There's no law in Dunstan. Oley Olsen's word don't mean doodley squat to Fisher or the mayor. And I haven't found the rifle that matches the cartridge Dog found. All I know, it's Fisher's gun."

The hound was nestled as close to Sam as he could get. He stuck out a long tongue and licked his hand.

Beaver said, "First things first. You say the two bad uns may be somewhere twixt here and Dunstan?"

"Could be."

"Iffen they made camp there'd be a fire."

"See what you mean."

"May work, may not. If we got 'em and the boy that got beaten talks, mebbe it'll stir up somethin' in town. You say the mayor ain't all bad."

"It's his son did the dirt."

"Still and all. Nothin' ventured nothin' gained."

"Okay." Sam petted the shaggy head and tightened the cinch on Midnight and restored the bridle. They rode down to the road, Dog trotting along at the heels of their mounts.

They were halfway to Dunstan when Beaver sniffed the air. "Smoke to the right."

They rode into a small bunch of trees and tied up. Dog was ahead of them going up the hill, nose quivering, pointing. Uncanny as usual, Sam thought, the hound always seemed to anticipate the action.

The campfire was imprudently high, visible at too great a distance for safety. Beaver and Sam separated and crept through foliage and between rocks. They came upon the pair simultaneously, Sam with his gun in hand.

The two young men sat agape, their hands raised. There was no question in Sam's mind as to their identity but he snapped, "Monty. Doodles or whatever your name is. Don't make a move. Not even your little fingers."

"Uh . . . yessir, Mr. Jones," stammered the one called Doodles. Monty did not lose his malignant stare as Beaver came in behind him and removed his revolvers from their holsters.

Sam said, "Take his belt, too. You may need a short gun."

Beaver obeyed, saying, "Never had any use for these but there's allus a day." He went to Doodles and unbuckled a fancy, tooled belt and draped it over his arm. "Should we hogtie this pair?"

Sam could see Oley Olsen lying in the bed with his distorted features, his bruised body. The anger boiled in him. "Which one of you held the boy while the others hammered on him?" he demanded.

"I dunno what you're talkin' about," Monty said, sullen, defiant. Doodles hunched his shoulders. Dog growled at them. Beaver stood silent, one gun in his right hand.

They had built the fire on a small table of land. Sam slowly unbuckled his belt and put it on the ground. Dog stood over it, fangs bared. Both the youths were about Sam's size, each probably heavier. He faced them, the anger beginning to spill over.

He said, "All right. I'll make a deal. If you two can beat up on me you can go free. Otherwise you talk and talk straight."

Without warning Monty leaped, swinging a fist. Doodles was slower. He dove at Sam's legs. Dog moved but Beaver said, "No! Stay down."

269

Sam swayed, evading the punch. He kicked and caught Doodles alongside the head, sending him sprawling. Always careful of his hands he dug an elbow into Monty's neck, spinning him.

Doodles had fallen into the fire. Howling, he flew staggering back to Sam. Recovering, Monty came low, head-first, knocking Sam off balance.

Doodles got in the way, swinging wild punches. For a moment Sam was buried beneath the two of them.

He kicked his way free. He caught Doodles by the nape of his neck and shoved him against Monty. They threw wild punches, managing only to hit each other. Sam grabbed Doodles by the arm and wrenched. There was a loud howl of pain and Doodles fell away.

Sam finally had to punch. He used his left hand, sending a crushing blow to Monty's middle. As the head went down Sam's knee came up. Monty did a back somersault and lay still.

Doodles, holding his right arm with his

left hand, cried, "I give up! You broke my arm!"

Monty was unable to speak.

Beaver said calmly, "Never did believe in fair fist fightin'. You mighta got hurt, friend."

Sam said, "They didn't have anybody to hold me." He was still steaming. "You, Doodles, or whatever. Tell me about it."

"About what?" Doodles was sniveling.

"About Oley Olsen."

"It was the Kid's notion. We'd been drinkin'. The Kid did most of it."

"I see. You just stood by."

"It was the Kid," he insisted. "Well, Monty likes to hit people. He hit me a lot when we was growin' up."

On the ground, recovering his senses, Monty growled, "You pusilatin' booby, shut your damn mouth."

"Maybe you'd like to talk?" Sam asked him.

Dog growled, showing his teeth, his muzzle close to the face of the youth on the ground. Monty flinched, showing the first sign of fear.

271

"Get that mutt away from me."

Sam said, "For two pins I'd let him eat your black heart out. It'd probably poison him. Brave sons o' bitches, you three. Real brave. If I don't see you in jail I promise you I'll see you in hell."

Doodles wailed, "We didn't kill him. . . . Did we?"

"That's what you're going to find out," Sam told him. "Right now you two saddle up. Please make a wrong move and give me an excuse to drill you."

He donned his belt and watched them put the saddles on their horses. He put out the fire. Dog kept hungry eyes upon their every move. Beaver emptied the cartridges from their gun belts and stuffed as many as he could into his dangling buckskin pouch. He shoved the two short guns into his belt, right and left, grumbling all the time that he preferred a rifle "when a man kin see what he's shootin' at."

"You got a rifle on your saddle," Sam said. "If these two try to run you can use it."

"They won't run. One's scared Dog'll git him, t'other's just plain scared."

He was telling the truth, it seemed, as they rode down the main road. Doodles still complained but his arm was not broken. Monty relapsed into sullen silence. Dog followed closely behind the two prisoners with Sam and Beaver bringing up the rear. The moon had come to full, shedding a ghostly light upon the caravan.

Beaver said, "Kinda like two Dan'ls ridin' into the lion's den, ain't it?"

"Might be more like two lions ridin' in to eat a town."

"You're countin' a heap on Cy Dunstan."

"There's decent people everywhere," Sam said.

"Seems like there's more of the other kind where we're headed."

"True. You got any notions?"

Ahead of them Dog suddenly stopped, nose pointing, tail out straight as a clothesline. Beaver swung down from the mule. Sam called to the prisoners to rein in. Beaver put his ear to the ground.

"Hosses comin' this way," he said.

"Into the trees," Sam ordered. The two obeyed. Beaver remounted. Dog followed as they pulled into a growth where they could not be seen from the main trail.

Sam said, "You two. Make a sound and you're where you ought to be, in hell."

Doodles inhaled sharply, biting at his lip, his grin long faded. Monty sat like a stone. Sam drew his gun and showed it. "I'm thinkin' of Oley right now."

All was still as a light breeze blew. The moon shone without fear or favor upon the just and the unjust.

They came, Fisher and the others. They were riding slowly, on the alert, scanning both sides of the road. They were looking for the pair now under guard and for Sam himself, he thought. It was tempting to attack, to send Monty and Doodles down to provide a diversion and to come in behind them with guns blazing.

It was not a good idea, he decided.

Better to remain behind them and try to do something in town.

Fisher turned his face toward the trees where they were hidden. Sam pushed his revolver beneath Monty's ear. Dog growled deep in his throat and went on point again. Fisher waved his arm and the coterie moved on.

When they were out of hearing Beaver said, "That hound's got somethin' agin Fisher. You see it?"

Monty muttered, "Dirty damn dog."

"What's that mean?"

Monty shut his mouth tight.

Sam turned to Doodles. "You want to say somethin'?"

He whined, "I need the doctor for my arm. The dog was around, got under Cap's feet."

"He shoulda shot him then," Monty growled. "He woulda, too."

Sam said, "I bet he would. Shall we ride to town?"

"I need the doctor," Doodles was wailing.

275

"You'll need him worse before this is over," Sam promised. "Vamoose!"

By now Sam knew the back ways of Dunstan almost as well as he knew those of Sunrise. He brought the little calvacade to the rear of the Olsen residence without incident. He tapped on the door and Sven answered, rifle at the ready.

Sam said, "Whoa, it's only me and a couple of bastards. And a friend."

"You got them? Lemme at 'em."

"Not the way to do it. Besides I marked 'em up some for you. How's Oley?"

Sven relaxed noticeably. "Settin' up. The doctor's here. Come on in."

In the bedroom Oley lifted one hand. "Mr. Jones."

Sam said, "Hey, this is great."

Cassie said, "Thanks to Doctor Fox. Thanks to the good Lord."

Sam said, "Anything I should know?"

The young doctor said, "They are actually holding one of Miss Brazile's dancing lessons. However, few will attend."

"Doc spread the word. Told 'em to keep away," Cassie said.

"Mayor Dunstan does not own my practice," Dr. Fox said.

"Even those who owe him wanta give the mayor the message," Sven said.

"Kid Dunstan?" Oley's voice was weak.

"No. Got the other two."

"Monty and Doodles." Oley moved, showed pain, ceased.

"Like you said. Want to plant 'em here for a spell. Youall got to promise not to kill 'em."

"I could render them unconscious for several hours," said the doctor.

"I like your style, Doc," Sam said. "I'd rather have 'em so that one or the other of them can squeal. We'll truss 'em up and they can think about the bind they're in. Can we use your barn?"

"Wish I could help." Oley managed a grin.

Cassie said, "My goodness, you and your friend must be hungry."

"Just for a nibble. But I got a hound

out there could eat one o' your horses and ask for more."

"There's plenty of meat in a butcher's house," Sven told him. "Can you stay, Doc?"

"I'd be obliged. One town, one medical man. Tires a fellow out."

Sven led the way outdoors. He paused when he saw the three waiting horsemen, then went on. He lit a lantern in the stable. There was a coil of rope on a wooden peg.

Sam said, "You can watch but don't kill."

Sven nodded, his face hard as agate. Beaver, Dog following, ushered the pair into the barn and said, "Learned about knots from the Injuns. Lemme do this."

Sam stood beside the twin and gently held his arm, feeling the tremor of rage in the young man, recognizing it. "Easy."

Beaver said, "You two, down on your faces."

The prisoners stared at Sven and Sam. Now Monty showed emotion, swallowing hard. Doodles was close to tears. Neither spoke as Beaver began to do tricks with the rope. When he had finished, in no time at all, the pair were face down, knees bent behind them, a strand of the rope connecting their legs with a wipe around their throats. It they tried too hard to escape they would strangle themselves, Sam saw. He went to them, took their bandannas from them and gagged each, showing no mercy. He said, "Maybe you'll have company later. Maybe your pardner will join you. Keep it in mind; it'll make you feel better."

Sven said, "You marked 'em up some. Not enough, though."

"Best we leave them and eat and think this out."

Beaver said, "Best idee yet today."

Dog growled in his throat. They doused the light in the barn and went into the house.

Mrs. Liz Dunstan was saying, "Now, Danny, you know your pa said you can't have any money."

He was sweating. "Mama, I owe it."

"Why are you so squirmish? We're just goin' to the dance lesson, all of us."

"I got to pay a man what I owe. Please, Mama."

She dug into her reticule. "Well. Twenty dollars. Now don't you let your pa know I give it to you."

"He'll never know. I gotta run, Mama."

"Gimme a kiss."

He touched her cheek with his dry lips and ran out to the stable. He had a horse saddled in readiness. He was scared to pieces; he could not stay alone on the ranch, and he feared going into town. He saw Tom Vaughn in the bunkhouse and got away as quietly as he could manage. He spurred the horse into a dead run for town.

He dropped from the horse behind the whorehouse and went to the back door. Kate regarded him with cold indifference. He took out the twenty dollars and threw it in her lap.

"I wanna know anything you heard

about Cap Fisher or any other thing that's happenin'."

She said, "He's gone with his riders to the north. You got other matters to worry about."

"What d'you mean?" His stomach seemed to drop a foot.

"Beatin' up the Olsen twin. Every soul in town knows what you and them two did."

"What . . . what two?" Now his mind was reeling.

"You can't do nothin' in this town it don't git around. Hell, how d'you think I know Cemetery Jones is in town?"

"Jones? In town?"

"You better look out, sonny boy. Your pa may own us all but Cemetery Jones don't give an owl's hoot. He's got Doodles and Monty put away somewhere and he'll be on your ass."

The Kid swallowed hard, stared at her for a moment, then ran back to his horse. He rode the back yards to the saloon where he and the other two had become drunk. He said, "Put somebody on a horse and send 'em after Cap Fisher. Tell him that Cemetery Jones is in town. In town, understand? In town!"

The barkeep said, "That'll cost you twenty."

"I ain't got it on me. Put it on my bill."

"If it goes on the bill it's forty."

"I don't give a damn. Get a man out there right now or you might get it like some others."

The bartender said, "It'll be done. Nobody in this part of town's got any use for Jones."

Kid Dunstan said, "See word gets to the right people," and ran to his horse and rode to the City Hall. He tied up behind it at the farthest possible point so that he might get away on the moment. Not that he knew where he would go except back to the home ranch. Even there he would not be safe, he knew.

He arrived at the front of the building in time to see the family carriage arrive with his parents and Vera Brazile. He went to it and the dancing teacher handed him a rifle, saying in a low voice, "Take care of this. It belongs to Captain Fisher."

Kid Dunstan followed them into the hall. The lights were already on and the black men were on their little dais with their instruments. There was no one else in the place. He leaned the gun behind the bandstand. His father was half drunk and all the way angry.

"By damn, where is ev'body? It's time they were here. By gum I give 'em the best in the West and they don't appreciate it. I'll have some hard words for them that don't show up and you can tell the world right now."

Mrs. Dunstan asked, "Who is there to tell? Ain't nobody."

Vera Brazile said in a patient, silken tone, "Now, folks. Let us be patient. They will probably arrive soon. Pompey! Play."

Music wouldn't do it, Kid Dunstan thought. Everyone knew about Oley

Olsen. He put his hands in his pockets but the shaking did not stop.

It was deceptively quiet in the Olsen house. Cassie fed soup to Oley with a large pewter spoon. The hound chewed on a bone in the kitchen. Sven, Sam, and Beaver, replete with steak and potatoes, gathered in the bedroom. The doctor lingered. Sam spoke to him.

"Could you stick around here for a spell?"

"I could. I will."

"You and Cassie can hold the fort. I know Sven won't stay still any longer."

The twin's hand crept to his gun butt. "You said that right."

"Let's augur. Sooner or later Fisher's goin' to find out we're in town," Sam said.

"He's always got somebody snoopin' around," Sven agreed.

"So he ain't dumb. He'll be ridin' back. Meanwhile we want Kid Dunstan."

"Most of all," said Sven and Oley together.

"His father can't go against the truth," Sam continued. "Leastways I don't believe he can."

"His ma can," Cassie said.

"We take the chance Dunstan won't be shamed in his own town. Now I heard from the musicians that there might be one of their dances tonight."

Beaver said, "If they ain't to home they're at the hall."

"Only one way it could all go wrong," Sam said. "If Fisher, knowin' we're here, decides to go to Sunrise."

Beaver said, "He'll run himse'f into a buzz saw if he does. Whole town's awaitin' for him."

"We can hope on that. We got to."

Sven said, "Cap'll have a mean bunch with him."

"Sure he will." Sam grinned without mirth. "Countin' on that. Hope they had to do with tryin' to kill Renee."

"The three of you against all of them," Cassie said.

"I don't want anybody hurt account of me," Oley said weakly.

"Me, I got other reasons," Sam said.

"There will be some from the lowdown part of town will back Fisher," warned the doctor.

"Got to chance that," Sam said. Dog came in from the kitchen, licking his chops. "We forgot him."

Dog said, "Woof."

"He's been sorta lucky," Sam explained.

"Like a ha'nt," Beaver said.

"Palaverin' won't get it done," Sam said. "We leave the long guns, won't need 'em in this rangdoodle." He tried to make it as light as possible, seeing the worry on the faces of Cassie and Oley. The doctor seemed composed, a man of parts. Sam walked to the door.

Cassie and Oley waved goodbyes. Sven paused to touch his brother's hand and pat the girl's shoulder. They went out into the moonlit night.

Somewhere between Sunrise and Dunstan a rider stared curiously at a strange vehicle, then went on his way. In the imitation Conestoga wagon Adam Burr clucked at the big, sturdy dappled horse and said, "This is slow going."

Clayton Lomax said, "It's the wise thing to do."

"I know. It was a good idea. But Sam could be killed before we get close."

From behind them, seated on the bench, Renee said, "That's why we're here."

"Yes. He would never send to Beaver for help if he wasn't in grave danger," Adam assented. "But you, Clay, you needn't have come along."

"Friendship," the preacher said. "Friendship is to be prized above all else on this earth. Sam Jones is your best friend. Sunrise has shown me friendship. It adds up."

"It might be very rough—and you won't fire a gun."

In the reflected light of the moon Lomax opened and closed his huge hands. "I have these."

"That's all I had when I came west. It was Sam taught me to use a revolver.

It was Sam who made me a confirmed westerner," Adam said.

Renee sat with her long hands clasped. It had been her idea to borrow the wagon and attempt to reach Sam. The response from Adam had been immediate and the preacher had joined them at the last moment. They could have brought Donkey Donovan, she knew, but the presence of an outside lawman might have complicated matters even further.

Sam believed the danger came from Dunstan, therefore no doubt existed in her mind. Sam's instincts in the presence of danger were not to be debated. Sam had dwelt on the precarious edge of danger for years—too many years, she thought. That was what worried her so much, the apprehension that his fortune would change. If he was to die in her defense, she wanted no more than to die with him. It was a sobering thought, one hitherto strange to her.

Adam said, "Better we should be moving than waiting. The suspense was too much after Beaver left."

Renee said, "I wish Peggy had stayed home." There was a slight swerve to the road and a shaft of moonlight touched the sleeping girl on the built-in cot. The hard life had left no marks upon Peggy McLaine Burr. Young and pretty, she had the resilience and courage of her grandfather, Renee thought. There had been no way they could leave her behind. Adam said as much now. The big horse continued its steady, space-eating pace. Renee sank into deep thought.

The rider Kid Dunstan had ordered to be sent said, "He's back in town's all I know."

Maguire said, "The bastid moves like a damn ghost."

"All the better," snapped Fisher. "We'll nail him in town."

"You ask me, we oughta go on to Sunrise and finish the job."

Fisher said in a fierce whisper, "Shhh! That's between you and me."

"It's the main job. Without Jones we can do it."

After a moment Fisher shook his head. "With him still alive we'll never see a day we don't expect him."

"What the hell?" Maguire had lived that way all his grown existence.

The other men sat their horses and paid little heed to the dialogue. They were hired to follow, not to make decisions.

"These four tried it on Jones," Maguire said, nodding toward them. "Lotsa people tried it on him. Right now them dumb bastid kids got him riled. No tellin' what he's up to."

"He'll be at the dance lesson," Fisher said. "He'll be raising a fuss over the beating of the Olsen twin."

"The mayor's on the hot seat," Maguire said. "His kid and all. I say let that rest and we go to Sunrise."

"We can charge Jones. We know he'll fight. He won't have a chance."

"Mebbe not. But some of us got to die in a fight with him. How do we know which?" Maguire grinned, his thin face a ghoulish mask in the light of the moon.

"He don't know me personal. He knows you."

"I'll take the chance."

Maguire said, "Look, I rode myself skinny on this job. I put up with that scum Rafferty and slept no more'n an hour or two in Mexican smells. This here ridin' into a town that's not expectin' us is the best dodge we had yet. What've they got? A marshal and one deputy. A few storekeepers, a couple cowboys. I can rouse Rafferty to help with some men. I want this job ended."

"You've been paid plenty," Fisher said.

"What good's money when you're dead?"

"Are you scared of Jones?"

"Scared? Certainly I'm scared. You ain't scared to face Jones you're a damn fool."

"Then I'm a fool."

"Could be," Maguire told him. "Me, I ain't no fast gun. I'm a man does nasty jobs for people so he can gamble and live in whorehouses. I stay alive bein' scared of shooters like Cemetery Jones."

Fisher shook his head. "We're different. I'd rather go down facing him. It's a matter of principle."

"With you it's whatever you say." Maguire lifted a thin shoulder. "With me it's stay alive and enjoy life. Hey, you're the boss."

Fisher considered. The man's pure sophistry was a bit tempting. On the other hand he had his own goal to consider above all. He had felt the gap between Vera Brazile and himself growing day by day. He had needed her money. Now perhaps he could be free of that necessity by taking over Dunstan . . . or at least the policing of the growing town while he waited a chance to dethrone the present boss. It was his opportunity to acquire power, that lifetime desire. If he could accomplish the other deed and obtain more money from the woman who hated Renee Hart with such passion so much the better. Meantime he must temporize with this grinning, evil employee.

"Riding into Sunrise with these few men is more dangerous than facing Jones. Can't you see that? They are warned. They are on their own ground. Dunstan is our home ground."

"Like I said. It's up to you."

One of the men waiting up ahead called, "There's a wagon comin' down the road. Sort of a canvas top rig."

"Better we're not seen," Fisher said. "Back to town, men. You all want Jones. Let's get him."

They wheeled their horses and rode. Maguire dropped back to the tail end of the group, which did not go unnoticed by Fisher. If the man was going to skulk it was well to be warned, he thought. Still, if there was a chance to put a bullet in the back of Cemetery Jones, he was fairly well assured that Maguire would be on the job. Jones alone in Dunstan—that was the key. Fisher's confidence grew as he rode. He did not give a thought to the canvas-covered wagon winding its way to Dunstan.

Sam, Beaver, and Sven crossed the dark yard behind the Olsens' house.

Sam said, "We better pick up our customers in the barn and go."

Sven led the way with the lantern. Dog jumped ahead as they entered the barn, growling at Monty.

The two were gasping at their efforts not to contract their legs. Beaver reached down and loosened the connecting link of rope and they groaned as their legs extended.

"Their hands behind 'em will do," Sam said.

Doodles moaned, "My arm. It's dead."

"You're lucky the rest of you ain't dead," Sven exploded.

"Now, now, just give us time," Sam said. "We have to get these jaspers in shape to take a walk right this minute."

Hands secured behind them they walked up and down, prodded by Sven's gun, Doodles protesting, Monty glowering, defiant. When their circulation had been restored Sam said, "Now we go to the dance."

"Damn you to hell," Monty snarled.

"Could be arranged," Sam said. "Thing is, you go along for the ride."

Dog snapped at Monty's heels. He flinched, muttering curses. Sam lined them up, prisoners to the fore, Sven directly behind them. He said to Beaver, "You want to be in this parade?"

"Best I lay low."

"Right. Me and Dog, we'll march behind," Sam said.

They paraded up the alley. Cassie and Dr. Fox saluted them from the window. It was, Sam thought, a matter of timing. Showing themselves on the main street had its danger but it was a chance to evaluate the response of the decent folk in Dunstan.

Hidden from view there were staring eyes as they made their way to the auditorium behind City Hall. Sam could feel them. Monty attempted to swagger; Doodles limped, shoulders bent. Sven prodded them. Dog sniffed the air as if estimating the possibility of an attack.

There was no way of knowing the whereabouts of Fisher and whatever force he had gathered. There was no way to estimate the reaction of Cyrus Dunstan to the evidence against his son. It was a matter of taking a chance and being ready to fight. And it still did not lead directly to the plot to assassinate Renee.

"It's a puzzlement," he said to Dog. "A damn tricky matter any way you figure."

The dog made a sound that had become familiar, a reassurance, Sam felt. They neared their destination and he could hear the music. It was lively. They would be dancing, whoever had finally attended the lesson.

Beaver had vanished from view. Doodles and Monty lagged. Sven shoved them toward the side entrance of the hall. Sam peeked in the window. The moon was at full, casting an eerie sheen upon the scene.

Inside the hall there were a half dozen

middle-aged or better couples, Vera Brazile, the older Dunstans—and the son and heir. They were moving, with little or no grace, at the instructions of the dancing teacher. There was no joy among them.

The music was loud and clear and good. Sam paused a moment to enjoy it. Sven pushed the captives to the door. Sam nodded and the twin opened the door and shoved Monty and Doodles inside.

The action was so swift that Sam could not get past the trio; then Dog collided with Sam's legs and immobilized him.

Kid Dunstan spun away from the stout woman he was unwillingly escorting and was out the back door faster than he had ever before moved. The only way to stop him would have been to shoot and Sam had no notion of doing so. When Dog started in pursuit, Sam called to him to stop. "Later, maybe," he said. "This here is good enough for right now."

Sven mourned, "I could've had him. If

you didn't tell me not to, I could've had him."

Now everyone was staring at them and the music stopped. Sam waited another minute, then said, "Seems like your son don't want to be in on this, Mayor."

"What the hell's goin' on here? What you doin' with those boys tied up like o' that?" Dunstan's voice was not quite so loud and forceful as it might have been.

Mrs. Dunstan was crying, "Danny! Where's my Danny gone?"

"Where the good people won't find him right now," Sam said.

"I wanta know." Dunstan's voice diminished. "You, Monty. What's this here about?"

Monty shrugged without speaking. The mayor stared at Doodles, who began talking as though a faucet had been turned on.

"It was your own son that started it. It was Danny Dunstan. He wanted to beat on Oley Olsen. He talked me into it. It was Monty held him. . . ."

Monty jerked on their bonds so that he

knocked Doodles off balance. "The hell with it," he growled. "Shut your fool mouth. The hell with the whole damn business."

"Oley Olsen is badly hurt," Sam said. "What are you going to do about these two? And your son?"

Mrs. Dunstan wailed, "They're lyin'. Danny wouldn't do any such thing."

"He did! He did too!" Doodles had fallen completely apart. His eyes were red, his face puffed, his shoulder hunched to relieve the pain in his arms. "If I hadn't been drinkin' I wouldn't of been in on it. It was the Kid and Monty drug me."

The small assemblage was drifting apart. The elderly people huddled together, staring accusingly at the Dunstans. The dancing teacher, oddly, had stationed herself beside the bandstand. The musicians were frozen into place, small, secret grins on their faces.

Monty thrust his unshaven dark jaw forward and demanded, "What right's this stranger got to arrest me? I ain't sayin' nothin'. The Kid ain't here to say anything. This here ain't legal, you hear me?"

Sam said, "Mayor Dunstan, you put the law in the hands of Captain Fisher. These jaspers worked under him. I don't see him around to take charge."

Dunstan said, "I'm the law around here. If what you say is the truth I'll attend to this pair."

"And your son?"

"My baby didn't do anything wrong." Mrs. Dunstan was at it again. "I don't care what anybody says."

"I got to hear both sides of this." Dunstan was now blustering.

Sven Olsen spoke up. "Oley said it was the Kid and these two. He said it the minute he woke up. They near killed him."

The hound made a sound in its throat. Sam suddenly wanted out of the bickering, out of the hall. His sixth sense was operating, far from the first time. The mayor was at a loss; it was best to leave the prisoners with him for the time being.

"I'll take care of these two. I'll talk with my son." Dunstan was shaken to his fancy dancing boots.

"I'll take your word for it," Sam said. He turned toward the door, taking Sven's elbow in his left hand. There was something wrong.

Kid Dunstan suddenly reappeared in the frame of the back door. He had a Winchester in his hands. His voice was a high soprano, fraught with unreasoning fear. "You let them two loose. You just cut them ropes. You hear me? I'll shoot you where you stand, Jones!"

Mrs. Dunstan screeched, "Danny, my boy," and ran into the line of fire.

The mayor roared, "Put that gun down you damn fool idiot!"

Kid Dunstan yelled, "Cap's a-comin'!" His father seized the rifle from him.

Sam said, "Outside."

Dog followed on his heels. Sven came along. They were in the moonlight in seconds. They heard Beaver say, "Comin' in. A heap of 'em."

They stood with their backs to the wall

as Fisher and his men rode into their vision. Inside the hall there was confusion. They could hear the mayor hollering, his wife beseeching. Out of the corner of his eye, as he stood beside the open door, Sam saw the dancing woman, who had been uncharacteristically silent, edge behind the bandstand out of sight.

Fisher's voice came clear and demanding from the shadow of the trees. "Sam Jones, you are under arrest."

"Better check with your boss," Sam called. He could not see the man.

"You're accused of assaulting Oley Olsen." Fisher became sonorous, righteous. "You will remain in custody until this is considered."

"Waugh! The man's pure outa his head," Beaver said. He was in the shadow of a big tree a dozen yards from where Sam, the dog, and Sven were standing. The hound now was growling in a manner Sam had not heard before, fierce as a mountain lion. He said, "Quiet, Dog, quiet." Still the growling went on, teeth bared, hair bristling.

Fisher said, "Babbit, you and your men secure the accused."

Babbit's loud voice replied, "Not me, Cap. Get his guns afore anybody tries him."

Inside the hall Mayor Dunstan was bawling at his son and the two whose hands were still tied.

Sam said to Sven, "Go in there and keep the story straight. Dunstan believes it now. Watch out for the dancin' woman, there's somethin' queer about her tonight."

The twin obeyed. Fisher was still trying to get someone to arrest Sam. Under the tree Beaver had a revolver in each hand. Dog was still making the ferocious sound in his throat. Sam made a fast decision. Sooner or later the legality of the situation would be forgotten and hot lead would fly in his direction. He made a quick jump and ran to where Beaver was covering him. Dog was with him every inch of the way.

Beaver said, "You mought be a bit off your head but you do move good. I'll be

303

hereabouts." He was gone again. Even the bright moonlight could not reveal his going.

Fisher called again in his best martial fashion. "Surrender or take the consequences."

There was a reason they had not attempted to shoot him down, Sam thought. "You know who beat Oley Olsen," he called, stalling for time. "Your boys know. Decent people know. The mayor knows. Your number's about up, ain't it, Fisher?"

Before there could be a reply the hound whirled, the tone of his growl becoming a recognizable warning. Sam wheeled around in the elongated slender shadow of the tree and fired his gun at a figure made silvery white by the moon. Maguire cried out and fell forward on his face.

"Still bushwhackin', eh, Fisher?" Sam made his tone as taunting as possible. "Why don't you come get me alone? I'll give you the chance. Call off your men. Try me." He took a wild shot. "Or is shootin' women your way?"

Fisher gave another order, "Dismount, men. Attack!"

From the north came Beaver's voice, "Bad medicine, pardner. The scum's a-comin'."

Now he heard marching feet. Beaver came closer and called, "Some son stirred up the rubbish. They got guns."

It was time to cut and run. Fisher's men were climbing down from their horses. A crowd of low-lifes from the rough part of Dunstan was gathering behind them. Sam had seen mobs at work before; they were of all human action the most terrifying.

There were people in the hall who would be endangered. The mayor himself, his son, and two confederates could be massacred to suit Fisher's ends.

Counting on confusion in the ranks of Fisher's men plus the advance of the mob from the low part of town he said, "Come with me Dog. We'll go to the dance."

Together he and the animal dashed back across the space which was moonlit as bright as day. Shots sounded. Lead whistled on the clear night air.

Sam and Dog lunged unhit through the door and into the auditorium. The scene was one of confusion. The middle-aged people were scurrying about looking for shelter where there was little or none. Doodles and Monty lay on the floor against the far wall. Mama Dunstan held onto her son, protecting him. Sven stood guard upon them all. Cy Dunstan, irresolute, for once without words, had his son's rifle in his hands. Vera Brazile peeked from behind the bandstand. The musicians sat as if entranced by the proceedings. The mayor said numbly, "I heard shots."

"You did. I had to kill a man," Sam told him. "Before it's over you may have to do likewise. Your man Fisher is, seems to me, takin' over."

Dunstan shook his head as if to brush off cobwebs. "What's that? What did you say there?"

"Listen." Sam gestured with his Colt. "He's plumb oratin'."

Dunstan went to the door. Fisher was saying in his dictatorial manner, "You want Cemetery Jones. He's in that hall. The mayor and his son are there. What did they ever do for you? It's time for a change, friends. You can come to me with your problems. I do not hold mortgages upon you. . . ."

Dunstan said, "The sumbitch!"

Sam asked, "Where's the dancin' lady?"

"Damn if I know."

"I'm here." She came forth dramatically, head high, carrying Fisher's rifle in her tiny hands. Sam had not before fully realized how small she was. She had the bearing of . . . an actress, he thought. He had seen them strut the stage in Dodge City, in his travels eastward. There was something unreal about her.

Dunstan said, "Fisher, the bastid."

"He's got half the town out there," Sam told them. "I've got a friend out there. One friend. And there's us. How do you like the odds?"

"I ain't got enough ammunition to hold

307

off no mob," said Dunstan. He was still at a loss, Sam saw.

"Wouldn't do us much good to have bullets against that many, now, would it?" he asked.

Vera Brazile's brows contracted. She stared at Sam. He saw through the veil then, saw hatred. The cog that had been missing in the machinery of his mind slowly moved into place.

He took two steps and said to her, "This will do better in the hands of somebody else." He took the rifle from her, surprised at her strength as she fruitlessly resisted. He handed it to Sven.

The twin broke it open. He said, "Hell, it ain't loaded."

"Let me see it." Sam turned the exposed hammer in the light of the moon through the window. The nick was plain to be seen. The burning anger gripped him once more. He turned savagely upon the woman. "Is this your property, lady?"

"It . . . it belongs to Captain Fisher," she said. "Mayor Dunstan can attest to that."

"That's right." Dunstan remembered what Sam had told him. "That the gun you're lookin' for?"

"The same. I'll be seein' your man Fisher."

"Not my man no more," Dunstan said. "No goddam puke like him."

"I hope we live to tell him about it." Sam had to live now. He had to face Fisher. Whatever else happened he had to get to the man for whom he had been searching.

He heard the voice again, "Surround the building. If they don't send out Cemetery Jones we shall go in and take him!"

Sam said crisply to Sven, "Keep one eye on that woman."

"The dancin' lady?"

"The same," Sam said. "Line her up with those other useless bodies against that wall."

Sven hesitated, then showed his gun to Vera Brazile. Her teeth flashed in a grimace at Sam, then she went silently to where Mrs. Dunstan huddled with the still bound pair of youths, her cowering son, and the innocent people.

Pompey came close to Sam and asked, "Miz Brazile, she one of the bads?"

"You can believe it." He would attend to her later. He did not know how he would do it but it had to be done, he knew. If he lived, that was, if any of them lived. He broke a pane of glass and peered out into the moonlight.

The mob had come in. They were like crawling dark animals as they came, carrying guns, knives, hatchets, clubs, whatever weapons they could command. They were as dangerous as wild animals, he knew. They were mindless, aching to do damage to make up for real or fancied wrongs. Many of them were drunk, or loaded with laudanum or opium. The danger could not be exaggerated.

He heard Fisher exultantly exhorting them. There was no way to stand against the numbers if they charged. A bullet whanged through the window close to his head. He fired blindly, rapidly. He heard cries that told him he had found targets. The air went out of the initial attack.

He said to Dunstan, "This won't do." Outside there were a couple more reports of a short gun he surmised was in the hands of Beaver. There were further yells from the mob. "Too many of 'em."

Dunstan was stunned, his voice an octave below normal. "Did I hear you say Vera's with 'em?"

"Is she close with Fisher? She had his rifle."

Dunstan said, "I hired him. Hired her, so to speak. Now my town is tryin' to kill me."

"Looks that way." Sam was reloading. He saw movement, emptied the sixshooter. "Not a good place to die."

"The town I built."

Sam said, "That gun of Fisher's. It's a .44. I got plenty ammunition for a .44 bore."

A fusilade burst through the window that Sven was watching, splattering harmlessly. The twin returned the fire.

Dunstan said, "Gimme that damn

gun." His voice rose to its normal volume. "I ain't goin' to die without a fight."

Sam said, "Didn't think you would, come down to it." He was again reloading, taking peeks at the situation. The moonlight held and he found a target, Babbit. The blusterer went down. There were shouts, shots, a few more groans. Fisher called for order, his voice fierce, demanding. The movement as of a pack of rodents slowed, melted into the shadows.

Now there was confusion indoors, at the back of the hall, demanding Sam's attention. The action was at Sven's post. His voice sounded, "I'll shoot!"

In the uncertain, diffused moonlight Sam saw bodies in action. Mama Dunstan cried out in anguish.

Then they were making for the door, Kid Dunstan, Doodles, Monty. In among them was Vera Brazile.

"Hold it," Sam called to Sven. Dog barked and stopped short at the heels of the fleeing group. Mayor Dunstan shouted to no avail.

Sam was at the window. He could find no targets. There was no one in sight. A fusilade of shots came from the shadows.

The escaping group went down like ninepins. They fell in a heap. As he watched, the dancing woman wriggled beneath the others, and he knew she had somehow evaded death.

The howling anger surfaced again in Sam. Dunstan was holding his screaming wife as she struggled to go to her son.

Without thought Sam slammed open the door and charged into the open.

There were no targets. The mob had seemingly evaporated. Astonishingly, Adam Burr's voice shouted, "Sam!"

Beaver echoed with a "Waugh. We got the devils!"

Into Sam's line of vision came the canvas-topped wagon belonging to Doc Bader. It was like a dream.

Fisher walked stiffly into the open as Sam holstered his gun. The man was white faced, grim.

He said, "Jones, what about it?"

"Comes down to us," Sam told him. "Take your shot."

Fisher's hand darted. He was fast.

Sam took a dancing step and drew. He shot Fisher neatly between the eyes. Fisher got off his shot. Behind him Sam heard a high, wailing cry. He turned to see Vera Brazile on her feet.

She took two steps, then flung her arms wide. Fisher's wild bullet had struck beneath her left breast. She staggered, fell to one knee. She coughed blood, mumbled a name Sam could not distinguish and died.

Adam, the new preacher, Beaver, Peggy and Renee were coming toward him. Behind them he caught a glimpse of Oliver Dixon and other citizens of Dunstan bearing arms.

Beaver said, "Waugh! The good people rose up."

Tom Vaughn and two cowboys from the Dunstan ranch rode into view. Sam waved at him and said, "You better take charge. There's plenty to set straight."

Then Renee was in his arms. The killing was ended.

They were in the hall where the dancing was now a memory. Bodies of the dead had been laid out in a row. Dr. Fox had done his best with the wounded.

Cy Dunstan said, "My son, he'll live. He may be a cripple, but he'll live. Jones, I seen what you did with Fisher. You want the job of marshal here you got it."

"No, thanks."

Renee called out, "Sam!" She was standing over the body of Vera Brazile. "What did you say was her name?"

He told her. She shook her head, shocked. "Her name is Katherine Jane Winslow. She's from New York City."

"You knew her?"

"Only from pictures in the newspapers and magazines. She was a ballet dancer. Wealthy. Then she was . . ." Her lips closed. She said no more, turning away.

"What's that?" demanded Dunstan. "That's the damnedest thing. What's it all about?"

Sam spoke, thinking fast, staving him off. "She and Fisher were a team, you see? They were goin' to take over your town one way or another."

"The hell you say. Were they the ones tryin' to kill you and your lady?"

"Fisher." Sam had to manufacture a story for Renee's sake. "I reckon he wanted to get me for some reason. Folks generally do. Missed me, botched the job, and I figured he was aimin' for her." It was getting difficult. "We'll never know for sure, will we?"

"The dead won't tell." Dunstan seemed satisfied for that moment at least.

Renee stood silent. The door to her past, open for a second, was closed again.

Dog was standing over Fisher's body, still growling. Sven Olsen said, "He ain't forgot the kick he got from Cap."

The musicians were together, waiting. Sam went to them and said, "It's all over but the burying. Will you take the stage to Sunrise for me?"

"What you wants, you get," Pompey told him. "Can we go home, then?"

"I'll pay your way to New Orleans."

"Anything you say, man from Sunrise."

Sam gathered his coterie of friends. "We got to see Oley and his gal."

As they were leaving he saw Tom Vaughn and three cowboys taking charge and knew that order would be restored and the odds and ends cared for. He waved as he departed the scene of music, dancing, and death.

Oley Olsen was sitting up. Cassie was holding his hand. When all had been introduced the girl said to Sam, "You say that tall man is a real, honest to goodness preacher?"

"He is."

Oley said, "We could use him."

Lomax came from the kitchen, swallowing cold meat. Sam said, "Seems like they need you to do a job."

Sven said, "Ma and Pa can't stop 'em from marryin' now. We owe you a heap, Sam."

"Nobody owes me anything," Sam said. "The town was there when it was needed. You still got mortgages but I got an idea old Cy won't be so tough from now on."

So the war in Dunstan was ended. The nicked cartridge would go into Sam's tack. It would never be proven who fired the shot at Renee. No one cared.

Philip Barnes Merrivale and his uncle sat in the opulent library again. New York bustled outside. There was another bottle of fine wine.

Uncle Barnes asked, "Did you see the Herald today?"

"Indeed. I checked to see from whence came the story."

"From the West, was it not?"

"Some sort of fighting in a western town. Danstone, or something like that. Imagine Katherine Winslow out there."

His uncle said, "She was a headstrong woman."

"We knew that. She made her own trouble, always."

They sipped the wine. Then the older

man said, "I firmly believe your love is also dead."

"No. If she were I would know."

"You repeat over and over that you would know. You cannot know."

"I can believe."

"Yes." The senator was silent for a moment. Then he said, "Bless you, my boy."

Philip Merrivale lifted his glass. Nothing further on the subject needed to be spoken.

It was evening at El Sol in the town of Sunrise. The musicians had been brought in on the stage. They were seated around the piano.

Missy said to Clayton Lomax, "I've never been in this place in my life before."

Her father said, "It won't harm you none, daughter. This here's a special event."

The dog lay between Renee and Sam. Beaver sat with the Burrs. Donkey and his deputy stood guard at the door.

Sam could not get his mind entirely off that which had transpired. He said to Renee, "Somebody in this town was tipping them off."

"I know."

"It could be most anybody. It bothers me a heap."

"Some day we might find out. Now is not the time."

He persisted. "Rafferty. I'll bet on it."

"So?" She smiled at him. She had completely recovered from her fears. "We're here. It's enough."

It was nearly enough but it left a thread loose. Pompey went to the piano. Sam said, "They want to go home to New Orleans. I promised 'em."

"We can't hold them. Let's listen."

They began to play. El Sol was so quiet that it was like church, Sam thought. They started out with the melody Sam remembered well, "The Saints Come Marching In".

Renee felt it in a jiffy, he knew without touching her. She responded immediately to the rhythm, the wailing of the horn, the deep richness of the violin. They played on.

When they stopped, hands clapped, glasses banged on tables and the bar. Sunrise had heard the sound of New Orleans and it would never be forgotten.

Dog stuck his muzzle up for petting. Sam obliged, watching Renee's fingers on the table trying to match those of Pompey. She would get it right, he knew. The new music had come to Sunrise, not Dunstan.

He wondered how the mayor and his wife were doing down there, knowing that their son was crippled, knowing the town was not theirs alone. He thought of the Olsens and Oliver Dixon and people like them. Some day, indeed, Dunstan might rival Sunrise.

That would be another day. He caught one of Renee's hands and held it as the music filled the saloon to overflowing. Dog muscled between them, demanding his share of attention.

ORPHAN'S PREFERRED
by Jim Miller

A boy in a hurry to be a man, Sean Callahan answers the call of the Pony Express. With a little help from his Uncle Jim and the Navy Colt .36, Sean fights Indians and outlaws to get the mail through.

DAY OF THE BUZZARD
by T. V. Olsen

All Val Penmark cared about was getting the men who killed his wife. All young Jason Drum cared about was getting back his family's life savings. He could not understand the ruthless kind of hate Penmark nursed in his guts.

THE MANHUNTER
by Gordon D. Shirreffs

Lee Kershaw knew that every Rurale in the territory was on the lookout for him. But the offer of $5,000 in gold to find five small pieces of leather was too good to turn down.

RIFLES ON THE RANGE
by Lee Floren

Doc Mike and the farmer stood there alone between Smith and Watson. Doc Mike knew what was coming. There was this moment of stillness, a clock-tick of eternity, and then the roar would start. And somebody would die . . .

HARTIGAN
by Marshall Grover

Hartigan had come to Cornerstone to die. He chose the time and the place, but he did not fight alone. Side by side with Nevada Jim, the territory's unofficial protector, they challenged the killers—and Main Street became a battlefield.

HARSH RECKONING
by Phil Ketchum

The minute Brand showed up at his ranch after being illegally jailed, people started shooting at him. But five years of keeping himself alive in a brutal prison had made him tough and careless about who he gunned down . . .

FIGHTING RAMROD
by Charles N. Heckelmann

Most men would have cut their losses, but Frazer counted the bullets in his guns and said he'd soak the range in blood before he'd give up another inch of what was his.

LONE GUN
by Eric Allen

Smoke Blackbird had been away too long. The Lequires had seized the Blackbird farm, forcing the Indians and settlers off, and no one seemed willing to fight! He had to fight alone.

THE THIRD RIDER
by Barry Cord

Mel Rawlins wasn't going to let anything stand in his way. His father was murdered, his two brothers gone. Now Mel rode for vengeance.

RIDE A LONE TRAIL
by Gordon D. Shirreffs

The valley was about to explode into open range war. All it needed was the fuse and Ken Macklin was it.

ARIZONA DRIFTERS
by W. C. Tuttle

When drifting Dutton and Lonnie Steelman decide to become partners they find that they have a common enemy in the formidable Thurston brothers.

TOMBSTONE
by Matt Braun

Wells Fargo paid Luke Starbuck to outgun the silver-thieving stagecoach gang at Tombstone. Before long Luke can see the only thing bearing fruit in this eldorado will be the gallows tree.

HIGH BORDER RIDERS
by Lee Floren

Buckshot McKee and Tortilla Joe cut the trail of a border tough who was running Mexican beef into Texas. They stopped the smuggler in his tracks.

HARD MAN WITH A GUN
by Charles N. Heckelmann

After Bob Keegan lost the girl he loved and the ranch he had sweated blood to build, he had nothing left but his guts and his guns but he figured that was enough.

BRETT RANDALL, GAMBLER
by E. B. Mann

Larry Day had the choice of running away from the law or of assuming a dead man's place. No matter what he decided he was bound to end up dead.

THE GUNSHARP
by William R. Cox

The Eggerleys weren't very smart. They trained their sights on Will Carney and Arizona's biggest blood bath began.

THE DEPUTY OF SAN RIANO
by Lawrence A. Keating and
Al. P. Nelson

When a man fell dead from his horse, Ed Grant was spotted riding away from the scene. The deputy sheriff rode out after him and came up against everything from gunfire to dynamite.

SUNDANCE: IRON MEN
by Peter McCurtin

Sundance, assigned to save the railroad from a murder spree, soon came to realise that he'd have to fight fire with fire, bullets with bullets and death with death!

FARGO: MASSACRE RIVER
by John Benteen

Fargo spurred his horse to the edge of the road. The ambushers up ahead had now blocked the road. Fargo's convoy was a jumble, a perfect target for the insurgents' weapons!

SUNDANCE:
DEATH IN THE LAVA
by John Benteen

The land echoed with the thundering hoofs of Modoc ponies. In minutes they swooped down and captured the wagon train and its cargo of gold. But now the halfbreed they called Sundance was going after it, and he swore nothing would stand in his way.

GUNS OF FURY
by Ernest Haycox

Dane Starr, alias Dan Smith, wanted to close the door on his past and hang up his guns, but people wouldn't let him. Good men wanted him to settle their scores for them. Bad men thought they were faster and itched to prove it. Starr had to keep killing just to stay alive.

FARGO: PANAMA GOLD
by John Benteen

Cleve Buckner was recruiting an army of killers, gunmen and deserters from all over Central America. With foreign money behind him, Buckner was going to destroy the Panama Canal before it could be completed. Fargo's job was to stop Buckner—and to eliminate him once and for all!

FARGO: THE SHARPSHOOTERS
by John Benteen

The Canfield clan, thirty strong, were raising hell in Texas. One of them had shot a Texas Ranger, and the Rangers had to bring in the killer. Fargo was tough enough to hold his own against the whole clan.

SUNDANCE: OVERKILL
by John Benteen

Sundance's reputation as a fighting man had spread. There was no job too tough for the halfbreed to handle. So when a wealthy banker's daughter was kidnapped by the Cheyenne, he offered Sundance $10,000 to rescue the girl.

HELL RIDERS
by Steve Mensing

Wade Walker's kid brother, Duane, was locked up in the Silver City jail facing a rope at dawn. Wade was a ruthless outlaw, but he was smart, and he had vowed to have his brother out of jail before morning!

DESERT OF THE DAMNED
by Nelson Nye

The law was after him for the murder of a marshal—a murder he didn't commit. Breen was after him for revenge—and Breen wouldn't stop at anything . . . blackmail, a frameup . . . or murder.

DAY OF THE COMANCHEROS
by Steven C. Lawrence

Their very name struck terror into men's hearts—the Comancheros, a savage army of cutthroats who swept across Texas, leaving behind a bloodstained trail of robbery and murder.